With a gasp, the little girl shrank back against Lad. The upper half of her body moved away from the danger. But her legs and feet lay motionless. . . .

With a cry of panic, The Child picked up a picture book from the rug beside her, and threw it at the snake. The book missed its mark. But it gave the copperhead reason to believe itself attacked.

Back went the triangular head. And then it flashed forward.

But before the snake could bite her, The Child was knocked flat by a mighty, furry shape lunging across her toward her enemy.

The copperhead's fangs sank deep in Lad's nose.

A Background Note about *Lad: A Dog*

Lad: A Dog takes place in northern New Jersey during the 1910s and 1920s. At that time, most people living in the area worked on farms. Unemployed men often stopped at these farms, asking for jobs. But some men would sneak onto the properties, hoping to steal cattle or equipment. Since there were no local police patrols, farmers often relied on dogs for protection.

At the same time, in nearby New York City, wealthy businessmen often bought expensive, thoroughbred dogs—not for their intelligence, service, or companionship, but for a certain "look" that was considered fashionable. Such thoroughbred dogs were raised under harsh conditions and exposed to terrible diseases—just so their owners could show them off like fashion accessories in fancy dog shows.

But when the United States entered World War I, many Americans felt it was their patriotic duty to make personal sacrifices to help the war effort. People cut back on personal luxuries. They gave any money they could save to buy food, clothing, and medical supplies for war victims and soldiers. Dogs also contributed to the war effort. On the battlefield, dogs bravely carried messages across enemy lines. At home, they participated in dog shows that raised money for relief organizations, such as the Red Cross. And at least one dog—Lad—was awarded a special medal of honor.

LAD
A Dog

Albert Payson Terhune

Edited by Ruth A. Rouff and Lisa Barsky

 THE TOWNSEND LIBRARY

LAD: A DOG

TP **THE TOWNSEND LIBRARY**

For more titles in the Townsend Library,
visit our website: **www.townsendpress.com**

Illustrations © 2010 by Hal Taylor

Note: This book has been edited to make it more
accessible to today's readers.

ISBN-13: 978-1-59194-215-3
ISBN-10: 1-59194-215-2

Library of Congress Control Number:
2009943316

Contents

CHAPTER 1

His Mate

Lad was an eighty-pound collie, a thorough-bred in spirit and in blood. He had inherited his gentle dignity from endless generations of purebred ancestors. He was also courageous and wise. His shaggy coat, set off by the snowy ruff and chest, was like orange-flecked mahogany. His tiny forepaws were silvery white. And who could doubt, after looking into his mournful brown eyes, that he had a soul?

Three years earlier, when Lad was not yet fully grown, Lady was brought to The Place. She arrived in The Master's overcoat pocket, rolled up into a fuzzy gold-gray ball no bigger than a kitten. The Master fished the month-old puppy out of his deep pocket and set her down on the veranda floor. Lad walked cautiously across the veranda and sniffed at the blinking pup, who dared to growl up at him so boldly.

From that first moment, Lad became Lady's protector. Then, as the shapeless yellow baby grew into a graceful collie, Lad's guardianship changed to pure adoration. He became Lady's slave for life. And she bossed the gentle giant in a shameful manner. She crowded him from the warmest spot by the fire, snatched the tastiest bones from his mouth, and pestered him into romping on The Lawn in hot weather, when he would much rather have dozed under the trees.

Lad joyfully put up with Lady's teasing, moodiness, and outbursts of temper. In Lad's eyes, all she did was perfect. And Lady, like many humans, enjoyed being idolized.

Life at The Place was wonderfully pleasant for both dogs. There were thick woods to roam in. There were squirrels to chase, and rabbits to trail. There was the ice-cool lake to plunge into for a swim, after a run in the July heat. There was a marvelously comfortable old rug in front of the fireplace to lie upon, shoulder to shoulder, on cold winter nights. Best of all, they agreed, there were The Master and The Mistress—especially The Mistress.

Any man with money may become a dog's owner. But no man may become a dog's Master unless the dog agrees. And once a dog accepts a man as Master, that Master becomes that dog's god. To both Lad and Lady, the man who bought them was not simply their owner.

He was the absolute master, the unquestioned lord of life and death, the eternal law. His was the voice that must be obeyed, whatever the command.

From earliest puppyhood, both Lad and Lady had been brought up by The Master to act according to The Law. As far back as they could remember, they had known and obeyed The Place's simple code. For example, they were allowed to chase all animals of the woods. However, they must ignore The Mistress's prize chickens and the other little creatures of The Place, no matter how much a collie felt like playing.

They must not bark, except as a friendly greeting, at any human who was walking openly or riding down the drive into The Place during the daytime. But they must attack on sight anyone sneaking onto the grounds.

Another law said that the inside of the house was sacred. It was a place for perfect behavior. No rug must be scratched. Nothing could be gnawed or played with. In fact, Lady's only whipping was for breaking this law. That was when, as a foolish puppy, she had tried to play with the huge stuffed eagle displayed in The Master's study.

The Master loved the eagle, which he had shot as it raided the flock of prize chickens. So after Lady played with it, he taught her a painful lesson that made her cringe for weeks afterward at the sight of the dog whip. To this day, she never walked past the eagle without taking the widest way around it. For Lady would no more have thought of playing with the eagle than a human would think to stand on his head in church.

Then, early one spring, Knave arrived at The Place. He was a showy, magnificent collie, with alert golden eyes and a coat that was reddish gold, except for a patch of black across his back. Knave did not belong to The Master, but to a man who asked him to care for the dog while he was away in Europe. The Master had willingly agreed.

When The Master arrived on the train from town, a crowd of people flocked to the baggage car to admire the fine-looking collie. But the grouchy old baggage man grumbled, "Maybe he's a thoroughbred, like you say. But have you ever seen a thoroughbred that had streaks of pinkish yellow on the roof of its mouth?"

Thinking such criticism silly, Knave simply yawned.

When The Master finally got off the train, Knave pulled joyously at the leash. As The Master reached The Place, both Lad and Lady came tearing around the side of the house to greet him. Upon seeing and smelling the strange dog prancing at his side, the two collies stopped short. Up went their ruffs. Down went their heads.

Lady crouched forward to battle the stranger, who was taking up so much of The Master's attention. Knave, who was quite willing to fight (especially with a smaller dog), braced himself and then moved forward, baring his fangs. But then he noticed that his enemy was a female. Suddenly his head went up, his lips relaxed, and his tail broke into swift wagging. Lady, noting the stranger's sudden friendliness, paused, uncertain. At that instant Lad darted past her and launched himself at Knave's throat.

The Master cried out, "Down, Lad! Down!"

The collie stopped his attack in midair. Though still furious, his only thought was to obey The Master.

Knave, seeing that Lad was not going to fight, turned once more toward Lady. "Lad!" ordered The Master. "Let him alone. Understand? Let him alone."

Lad understood. He must give up his impulse to make war on this hated intruder. It was The Law. And The Law must be obeyed.

Lad looked on with helpless rage while the newcomer was given the run of The Place. Sad and confused, he found himself forced to share with this intruder The Master's and Mistress's patting. It was painful to watch Knave playing with Lady, and Lady enjoying his attentions. Gone were the peaceful old days of simple and complete happiness.

Lady had always regarded Lad as her own special property to tease and to boss as she saw fit. But her attitude toward Knave was far different. Like a human girl attracted to a boy, Lady flirted with the gold and black dog. Sometimes she pretended to ignore him. At other times she met his advances with delighted friendliness. But Lady never tried to boss Knave as she had always bossed Lad. Rather, Knave fascinated her. Without seeming to follow him around, she was always at his heels.

Lady began to ignore Lad, which cut him to the heart. So Lad did everything he could think of to win back her attention. He tried to imitate the graceful way that Knave romped and found her rabbits to chase. But it was no use. Lady scarcely noticed him. When his attempts at friendship happened to annoy her, she rewarded them with a snap or an impatient growl. But she always turned to Knave, as if he had hypnotized her.

As Lady's total loss of interest continued, Lad's big heart broke. Being only a dog and having only noble thoughts, he did not realize that Knave's newness formed a large part of Lady's interest. Nor did he understand that such interest would surely fade in time. All Lad knew was that he loved Lady, and that she was snubbing him for the sake of a flashy stranger. But since The Law forbade him to fight for his Lady's love, Lad sadly withdrew from the unequal contest. He was too proud to compete for a fickle sweetheart.

No longer did Lad try to join in the others' romps. Instead, he lay at a distance, his splendid head between his snowy forepaws, his brown eyes sick with sorrow, watching Lady and Knave frisk about. Lad thought they didn't want him around. So instead of running with them in the woods, he stayed at the house and moped, alone and miserable.

From the beginning, Knave had scornfully ignored Lad. Since he did not understand that The Law did not allow the older collie to fight back, Knave looked down on Lad, assuming he was a coward.

One day, Knave came home from the morning run through the forest without Lady. Even though The Master called and whistled, Lady did not return to The Place. Lad slowly got up from his favorite resting place under the piano and trotted off to the woods. He did not return.

Several hours later, The Master went to the woods to investigate. Knave followed. At the edge of the forest, The Master shouted. Lad's bark answered from far away. Then The Master made his way through shoulder-deep underbrush in the direction of the sound. In a clearing he found Lady, her left forepaw caught in the steel jaws of a fox trap. Lad was standing protectively above her. Now and then he stooped to lick her foot, which was cruelly pinched in the trap. And he snarled at the hungry crows flapping in the treetops, hoping to attack the victim.

The Master set Lady free, and Knave frisked forward to greet her. But Lady was in no condition to play—not then, nor for many days to come. Her forefoot was so torn and swollen that for weeks she had to hobble on only three legs.

One pantingly hot August morning, Lady limped into the house in search of a cool spot, where she could lie and lick her throbbing forefoot. As usual, Lad was lying under the piano in the living room. His tail thumped a shy welcome as Lady passed. But she didn't even notice him.

On she limped, into The Master's study, where an open window sent a faint breeze through the house. Keeping her distance from the stuffed eagle, Lady hobbled to the window and started to lie down just beneath it. As she did so, she put too much weight on the sore foot and yelped in pain. At the same moment, a gust of air swept through the living room and blew shut the door of the study. Lady was a prisoner.

Ordinarily, Lady could have jumped out the window and onto the veranda, three feet below. But to make the jump knowing she would land on her injured forepaw—this was a feat beyond her willpower. So Lady accepted her imprisonment. Moaning softly, she curled up on the floor as far as possible from the eagle, and lay still.

At the sound of her first yelp, Lad ran toward her, whining sympathetically. But the closed door blocked his way. He crouched before it, miserable and anxious, helpless to go to his loved one's aid.

Knave, returning from a lone prowl of the woods, also heard the yelp. His sharp ears located the sound at once. He trotted up to the open study window. With a leap, he cleared the sill and landed inside the room. This happened to be his first visit to the study. The door was usually kept shut, so that breezes wouldn't blow around the papers on The Master's desk.

And Knave felt little interest in exploring the interior of houses. He was an outdoor dog, by choice.

Now he advanced toward Lady, his tail wagging, his head cocked to one side. Then, as he came forward into the room, he saw the eagle. He halted in wonder at sight of the enormous bird, with its six-foot wingspan. It was a wholly new sight to Knave. He greeted the eagle with a gruff bark, half of fear, half of bravado. Quickly, however, his sense of smell told him this wide-winged object was not a living thing. Ashamed of his momentary cowardice, he went over to investigate it.

As he went, Knave cast over his shoulder a look that invited Lady to join him. But the memory of that puppyhood beating made her shrink back. Knave thought, with a thrill, that Lady was actually afraid of this harmless thing. Eager to show off for her, and with an inborn craving to destroy, he sprang, growling, upon the eagle.

Down crashed the huge stuffed bird, Knave's white teeth buried deep in the soft feathers of its breast. Lady, horror-struck, whimpered in terror. But her fear only increased Knave's thirst for destruction. He hurled the bird to the floor, and tore the right wing from the body. Coughing out a mouthful of dusty feathers, he dug his teeth into the eagle's throat. Bracing himself with his forelegs on the carcass, he gave a sharp tug. Head and neck came away in his mouth. And then, before he could drop the mouthful and return to the work of demolition, Knave heard The Master's step.

Having destroyed The Master's property, Knave then showed his ignorance of The Law in a second way. In panic, he bolted for the window, the silvery head of the eagle still between his jaws. With a spring, he shot out through the open window, knocking against Lady's injured leg as he passed.

Knave did not pause at Lady's scream of pain. Nor did he stop until he reached the chicken house. There, he crawled under the floor, and deposited the telltale eagle head in the darkness. Then, finding no one following him, he emerged from the hiding place and jogged innocently back toward the veranda.

The Master heard Lady's cry as he entered the house. Recognizing from the sound that she must be in distress, he looked around for her. His eye fell on Lad, tense and eager, crouching in front of the shut door of the study.

The Master opened the door and went inside. At the first step inside the room, he stopped, amazed. There lay the chewed and battered remains of his beloved eagle. And there, in a corner, cowered Lady, looking frightened and guilty.

The Master was thunderstruck. For more than two years, Lady had been given free run of the house. What well-bred dog that had graduated from puppyhood would commit such a sin? He would not have believed it. He could not have believed it. Yet here was the terrible evidence, scattered all over the floor. The door was shut, but the window stood wide open. Without a doubt, she had gotten into the room through the window. And he had surprised her before she could escape by the same opening.

The Master was a just man, compared to most humans. But this was a crime even the most sentimental dog lover could not have excused. Moreover, the eagle had been his heart's pride. Without a word, The Master walked to the wall and took down a dog whip, now dust-covered from long disuse.

Lady knew what was coming. Being a thoroughbred, she did not try to run or roll for mercy. She cowered, motionless, awaiting her doom.

Back swished the lash. Down it came, whistling sharply. It struck with full force across Lady's slender flanks. Lady quivered all over. But she made no sound. Although she whimpered when her sore foot was accidentally touched, she was silent when punished by a human.

But Lad was not silent. As The Master's arm swung back for a second blow, a low growl came from behind him. The Master wheeled around. Lad was close at his heels, fangs bared, head lowered, tawny body taut in every muscle. The Master blinked at him, amazed. Here was something even more unbelievable than Lady's destruction of the eagle. Lad was threatening him. The Impossible had come to pass. For a dog might growl at its owner. But it would never growl at its master. Never.

Lad was miserable. For the first time in his life, his noble soul was torn between his two overpowering loves. He worshiped The Master, whom he had obeyed his entire life. But he loved Lady even more—poor Lady, who had been unjustly blamed and punished. In baring his teeth at his master, Lad knew he was breaking The Law in a way that was punishable by death. Yet still unflinching, he stood his ground.

The Master's jaw set. He was almost as unhappy as the dog. For he understood the situation, and he was man enough to honor Lad's sacrifice. Yet it must be punished, and punished instantly, as any dog master will swear. If a dog growls and shows his teeth at his master, the master must put down the rebellion at once, or lose his power over his dog forever.

Turning his back on Lady, The Master whirled his whip in the air. Lad saw the lash coming down. He did not flinch. He did not shrink away. The growl ceased. The collie stood erect. Down came the braided whiplash on Lad's shoulders, again over his sides, again and again.

Had a human other than The Master tried to strike him, Lad would have fought back. But now, with dark, tender, unblinking eyes, the hero dog took the whipping. When it was over, he waited only to see The Master throw the dog whip fiercely into a corner of the study. Then, knowing Lady was safe, Lad walked majestically back to his "cave" under the piano. With a long, deep sigh, he lay down.

Lad's spirit was sick and crushed within him. For the first time in his life, he had been struck. Like many dogs, Lad responded better to his master's words than to beatings, which caused humiliation, rather than pain. Through the numbness of his grief, Lad began to feel an overwhelming hate for Knave, the cause of Lady's humiliation. Lad knew what had passed behind that closed study door. For ears and nose tell a collie as much as its eyes.

The Master was as miserable as Lad. For he loved Lad as he would have loved a human son. Though Lad did not realize it, the reason The Master had stopped beating Lady was not to spare Lady's humiliation, but to spare Lad's grief.

The Master simply ordered Lady out of the study. As he watched Lady limp away, he was sorry he'd had to beat his favorite dog. He started gathering up the scattered pieces of the eagle, hoping he could still make a small trophy out of the fierce-eyed, silvery head. But he could not find the head. Then he remembered that Lady had been panting as she slunk out of the room. And dogs that are carrying things in their mouths cannot pant. So she could not have taken the head away with her. The missing head only deepened the whole annoying mystery. Finally, he decided just to give up trying to solve it.

At first, Lad felt so crushed and humiliated that he couldn't bring himself to risk a meeting with Lady. But after two days, he yearned for a sight of her. So he went out of the house in search of her. He traced her to the cool shade of a clump of lilacs near the outbuildings. There, Lady had dug a little pit in the cool earth with one paw and was curled up, asleep, under the bushes. Stretched out beside her was Knave.

Lad's spine bristled at sight of his enemy. But ignoring him, he moved over to Lady and tenderly touched her nose with his own. She opened one eye, blinked drowsily, and went to sleep again.

But Lad's coming had awakened Knave. Refreshed by his nap, Knave woke in a playful mood. He tried to encourage Lady to romp with him, but she preferred to doze. So, searching about in his shallow mind for something to play with, Knave remembered the prize he had hidden beneath the chicken house. Away he trotted, soon returning with the eagle's head between his teeth. As he ran, he tossed it in the air, catching it as it fell. This was a clever trick he had learned with a tennis ball.

Lad, who had lain down as near to Lady as he dared, looked up and saw his rival approach. Seeing what Knave was playing with made him mad. Here was the thing that had caused Lady's punishment and his own black disgrace. And Knave was boldly using it for his own selfish pleasure.

For the second time in his life, Lad broke The Law. In an instant, he forgot The Master's command to "Let him alone!" Noiselessly, terrifyingly, Lad flew at the playful Knave.

Just in time, Knave noticed the attack. He was mildly surprised that the dog he had looked down on as a coward should have developed a flash of spirit. But he was eager to wage a battle that would gain him more glory in Lady's eyes. Dropping the eagle's head, Knave sprang forward to meet his enemy.

Knave was three years younger than Lad and about five pounds heavier. Moreover, constant exercise had kept him in top condition. In contrast, lonely brooding at home had begun to soften Lad's tough muscles.

Like two furry whirlwinds, the collies spun forward toward each other. They met, reared up, and snarled. Like wolves, they slashed for the throat, while clawing madly to keep their balance. Then down they went, rolling in a savage embrace, snapping, tearing, growling. Lad went straight for the throat. But he missed the center, the only area of a collie's throat that isn't protected by a tangle of hair. A handful of Knave's golden ruff came away in his jaws.

Over and over they rolled. They regained their footing and reared again. Lad's saber-shaped fang ripped a gash in Knave's forehead. In return, Knave's half-deflected slash caused the big vein at the top of Lad's left ear to bleed.

By now, Lady was wide awake. Knowing she was to be the winner's prize, she watched every turn of the fight with wild excitement. Rearing up once more, the dogs clashed, chest-to-chest. Like one of his wolf ancestors, Knave dived for Lad's forelegs, hoping to break one of them between his foaming jaws. But he missed the hold by a fraction of an inch. Only the skin was torn. Down over the little white forepaw ran a trickle of blood.

That miss was a costly error for Knave. For Lad's teeth then sank deep into his enemy's left shoulder. Knave twisted and wheeled with lightning speed and with all his strength. Yet all his struggles would not have been enough to set him free. But then Lad started choking on Knave's fur, which stuck in his throat and blocked his nostrils. Gasping for breath, Lad relaxed his grip ever so slightly. And in that fraction of a second, Knave tore free, leaving a mouthful of hair and skin in his enemy's jaws.

The same motion that freed Knave also sent Lad stumbling forward. Knave saw his chance and took it. Flashing above his stumbling foe's head, Knave seized Lad from behind, just below the base of the skull. And holding him helpless, he began to grind his teeth in a slow, unstopping motion. Sooner or later he would chew down to the spinal cord and cut it in two.

Even as Lad thrashed about wildly, he felt there was no escape. He was nearly as powerless in this position as is a puppy held up by the scruff of the neck. Without a sound, but still struggling as best he could, Lad awaited his fate. No longer was he growling or snarling. His patient, bloodshot eyes searched longingly for Lady. But they did not find her.

Until now, Lady had been meekly awaiting the outcome of the battle. But then she saw the terrible jaws, grinding away the life of her old flame. Moved by some impulse she did not try to resist, she jumped forward. Forgetting the pain in her swollen foot, she nipped Knave sharply in the hind leg. Then, as if embarrassed by her unfeminine behavior, she drew back in shame. But the work was done.

Through the red war-lust, Knave dimly realized that he had been attacked from behind. Perhaps this new opponent stood a chance of gaining a death hold upon him. He loosened his grip on Lad, and whizzed about to face the danger. But before Knave had half-completed his lightning whirl, Lad had him by the side of the throat.

Though it was extremely painful, this was no death grip. Yet it held its victim just as powerless as Knave's jaws had just now held Lad. Bearing down with all his weight and setting his fangs firmly, Lad slowly shoved Knave's head sideways to the ground and held it there. Unable to break loose and in agony from Lad's grip on his throat, Knave lost his nerve.

The air vibrated with Knave's miserable howls of pain and fear. He was caught. He could not get away. Lad was hurting him terribly. And so he yelped like any cowardly mutt whose tail is stepped upon—rather than like a brave thoroughbred engaged in noble battle. The baggage man had been right about Knave's breeding.

After a while, beyond the fight haze, Lad saw a shadow in front of him, a shadow that soon became The Master. And Lad came to himself. He loosened his hold on Knave's throat, and stood up, groggily. Knave, still yelping, tucked his tail between his legs and fled for his life— and was gone forever from The Place, and from the story of Lad's life.

Stumbling, Lad slowly went up to The Master. The collie was gasping for breath, weak from exhaustion and loss of blood. Up to The Master he went, straight up to him. Not until he was barely two yards away did Lad see that The Master was holding something in his hand. It was that horrible, mischief-making eagle's head! Something was in the other hand— probably the dog whip. It did not matter much. Lad was ready for this final humiliation.

He would not try to dodge it, for now he'd twice broken The Law.

Suddenly The Master was kneeling beside him. The kind hand was stroking the dog's dizzy head. In a quivering tone, as if something were stuck in The Master's throat, the dear voice was saying remorsefully, "Oh Lad! Laddie! I'm so sorry. So sorry! You're—you're more of a man than I am, old friend. I'll make it up to you, somehow!"

And now, besides the loved hand, there was another touch, even more precious. It was a warmly caressing little pink tongue that licked his bleeding foreleg. Timidly, adoringly, Lady was trying to tend her hero's wounds.

"Lady, I apologize to you, too," went on the foolish Master. "I'm sorry, girl."

Lady was too busy soothing the hurts of her newly discovered mate to understand. But Lad understood. Lad always understood.

CHAPTER 2

"Quiet"

Everyone must have at least one god to worship. Lad had two: The Master and The Mistress. And because Lad was loving, and because The Mistress was very lovable, the collie worshipped her even more than The Master.

There were other people at The Place, whom Lad knew to treat politely. Often there were guests, too. Lad would shake hands with them, on request. He would even permit them to pet him. But as soon as he could, he always withdrew from their reach.

Of all the dogs on The Place, only Lad had the run of the house during the entire night, as well as during the day. Lad was allowed to sleep in his cave under the piano. He was even permitted into the dining room, where he always lay to the left of The Master's chair.

Lad was happy to go for a romp any time with The Master. And he would play like a puppy with The Mistress, rolling on the ground at her feet. But these two were the only ones who could approach him. From his earliest days, Lad never forgot he was a noble aristocrat. So, calmly aloof, he moved among his subjects, who were beneath him.

Then, all at once, Horror intruded into the peaceful routine of the house.

It began on a blustery October day. The Mistress had crossed the lake to the village in her canoe, with Lad curled up in the front. On the return trip, about fifty yards from shore, the canoe struck sharply against a half-submerged log. At the same time, a gust of wind caught the boat, spun it around, and tipped it over.

Both The Mistress and Lad splashed into the ice-cold waters. Lad bobbed to the top, and glanced around at The Mistress to learn if this were some new joke. But he instantly saw it was no joke at all. Weighted down by the folds of her heavy skirt, The Mistress was unable to swim toward shore. So the dog flung himself through the water toward her with a rush. In a second, he reached her and caught the shoulder of her sweater in his teeth. In this way, with Lad swimming mightily, they came at last to land.

Everyone rejoiced at what Lad had done, and Lad was quite proud of himself. He understood he had done a wonderful thing, and that all were trying to pet him at once. Lad wasn't used to so much handling and began to find it tiresome. At last, he retired to his cave under the piano to escape from it. Things soon quieted down, and the incident seemed to have ended.

Instead, it had just begun. For The Mistress had been stricken with a chill. And by night she was in the first stages of pneumonia.

Then gloom fell over The Place. A gloom Lad could not understand until he went upstairs to escort The Mistress to dinner. At first, there was no reply to his scratch at her door. So he scratched again, and soon The Master came out of the room and ordered him downstairs again. From The Master's voice and look, Lad understood that something was terriblywrong.

A strange man with a black bag came to the house early in the evening. He and The Master spent what seemed like an endless amount of time in The Mistress's room. Lad crept upstairs behind them and, still at their heels, tried to crowd into the room. But The Master ordered him back and shut the door in his face.

So Lad lay down outside the room and waited. He heard the murmur of speech inside. Once he caught The Mistress's voice, though it had a puzzling new note in it. So his tail thumped hopefully on the hall floor. But no one came to let him in.

The doctor almost stumbled across Lad as he left the room with The Master. Since he was a dog owner himself, he was not irritated. But it reminded him of something. "Those other dogs of yours outside there," he said to The Master, "raised an awful racket when my car came down the drive. Better send them all away somewhere till she is better. The house must be kept perfectly quiet."

The Master looked back up the stairway. There, Lad had pressed close against The Mistress's door. Something in the dog's heartbroken attitude touched him. "I'll send them over to the boarding kennels in the morning," he answered. "All except Lad. He and I are going to see this through, together. He'll be quiet if I tell him to."

All through the endless night, while the October wind howled, Lad lay outside the sickroom door. Sometimes, when the wind screamed its loudest, Lad would lift his head and growl. It was as though he heard, in the storm's racket, evil spirits trying to burst in and attack The Mistress.

Lad was there when day broke and when The Master, heavy-eyed from sleeplessness, came out of The Mistress's room. Lad was there when the other dogs were herded into the car and carried away to the boarding kennels.

Lad was there when the car came back from the station. It brought to The Place an angular, wooden-faced woman with yellow hair and a yellower suitcase. To Lad, she was a horrible woman, who smelled of disinfectants. The woman approached the sickroom, dressed in stiff white. Lad hated her.

Lad was there when the doctor came for his morning visit. Again the collie tried to edge his way into the room, only to be stopped once more.

Later that day, the nurse complained to The Master, whom she met at the top of the stairs. "This is the third time I've nearly broken my neck stepping over that miserable dog. Please drive him away from the door. I've tried to do it, but he only snarls at me. He should not be making noise when the patient is in such danger!"

"Leave him alone," ordered The Master.

But later, The Master called Lad over to him. Reluctantly, the dog left the door. "Quiet!" ordered The Master, speaking very slowly and clearly. "You must keep quiet. Quiet! Understand?"

Lad understood. Lad always understood. He must not bark. He must move silently. But at least, The Master had not forbidden him to snarl softly at that horrible woman every time she stepped over him. So that was one grain of comfort.

Gently, The Master called Lad downstairs, and put him out of the house. Three minutes later, Lad made his way through an open window into the cellar and then upstairs. Once again, he was stretched out at the threshold of The Mistress's room.

On his daily visits, the doctor was forced to step over Lad. But he was dignified enough not to curse. Twenty times a day, the nurse stumbled over the dog. And each time she fumed in helpless rage. The Master, too, came back and forth from the sickroom. Now and then he spoke a kind word to the suffering collie. And again and again he put the dog out of the house. But Lad always managed to be back on guard within a minute or two. And whenever the door of The Mistress's room opened, he tried his best to enter.

Servants, nurse, doctor, and The Master repeatedly forgot the collie was there, and kept stubbing their toes on his body. Sometimes their feet drove painfully into his flesh. But Lad never whimpered or growled. He had been commanded to be quiet, and he was obeying. And so it went on, through the awful days and the even worse nights. Except when Lad was ordered away by The Master, he would not stir from the door. And not even The Master could keep him away from it for long.

For days, Lad ate nothing, drank little, and did nothing except guard The Mistress's door. He longed to be inside the forbidden room to protect The Mistress from the unseen danger that was trying to take her away. But they would not let him in, these humans. That is why he lay there, pressing his body against the door, waiting. And, inside the room, death and the doctor fought their duel for the life of the still, little figure in the great white bed.

One night, the doctor did not go home at all. Toward dawn, The Master lurched out of the room and sat down for a moment on the stairs, his face in his hands. Then, and then only, did Lad leave the doorsill of his own free will. Shaky with hunger and weariness, Lad got to his feet and crept over to The Master. He lay down beside him, his huge head across the man's knees. After a while, The Master went back into the sickroom. And Lad was left alone to wonder and listen and wait. With a tired sigh, he returned to the door and once more took up his heartsick vigil.

Then one golden morning, days later, the doctor came and went with the look of a conqueror. Even the nurse forgot to grunt in disgust when she stumbled across the dog's body. In fact, she almost smiled.

After a while, The Master came out through the doorway. When he saw Lad, he stopped and turned back into the room. Lad could hear him speak. And then Lad heard a dear voice reply. The voice was very weak, but no longer had that muffled tone which had so frightened him. Finally came a sentence the dog could understand.

"Come in, old friend," said The Master, opening the door and standing aside for Lad to enter.

At a bound, the collie was in the room. There lay The Mistress. She was very thin and weak. But she was there. The dread Something had lost the battle. Lad wanted to break forth into a peal of overjoyed barking that would have deafened everyone in the room. But The Master read the wish and interrupted, "Quiet."

Lad heard. He controlled himself. But it cost him a world of willpower to do it. As calmly as he could, he crossed to the bed. The Mistress was smiling at him. She stretched out one weak hand to stroke him. And she was saying almost in a whisper, "Lad! Laddie!"

That was all. But her hand was petting him in the dear way he loved so well. And The Master was telling her all over again how the dog had watched outside her door.

As Lad listened to the woman's whisper, he quivered from head to tail. Although he desperately wanted to bark, he knew this was no time for noise. For The Mistress was whispering. Even The Master was speaking softly.

One thing Lad realized. The terrible danger was past. The Mistress was alive! And the whole house was smiling. That was enough. But the desire to show, in noise, his wild relief, was almost irresistible.

Finally, The Master said, "Run on, Lad. You can come back later." So the dog gravely made his way out of the room and out of the house.

The minute Lad was outdoors, he started to go crazy. Nothing but sheer insanity could excuse his actions during the rest of that day. Never before in his life had the collie misbehaved the way he did now. The Mistress was alive! The danger was past! Reaction set in with a rush.

The Mistress's moody gray cat, Peter Grimm, was picking its way across The Lawn as Lad emerged from the house. Ordinarily, Lad tolerated Peter Grimm. But now he dashed madly at the cat. Deeply offended, the cat scratched Lad's nose and fled up a tree, spitting and yowling, tail fluffed out as thick as a man's wrist. Seeing that Peter Grimm had scrambled up where he could not follow, Lad remembered the need for silence and did not bark threats at his escaped victim. Instead, he galloped to the rear of the house, where the dairy stood.

The dairy door was unlocked. With his head, Lad butted it open and ran into the stone-floored room. A row of full milk pans was standing on a shelf. Rising on his hind legs and bracing his forepaws on the shelf, Lad grasped each of the deep pans between his teeth. With a series of sharp jerks, he brought each one clattering to the floor. He stood there for a moment, ankle deep in a river of spilled milk.

Then Lad charged out into the open, where he saw a red cow, chained up in a pasture beyond the stables. She was an old friend of his, this cow. She had been on The Place since before Lad was born. Yet today, Lad tore straight at the astonished animal. In terror, the cow threw up her tail and tried to lumber away at top speed. But since she was chained, she could run only in a wide circle. So Lad drove the bellowing beast around and around in this circle until the gardener came to her relief.

But neither the gardener nor any other living creature could stop Lad that day. He next fled merrily up to the little lodge at the gate, burst into its kitchen, and yanked open the refrigerator. There, he found a leg of mutton. Taking this twelve-pound morsel of meat in his teeth, Lad dodged the angry housewife, raced outside, and dug a hole. He was cheerfully preparing to bury the mutton, when its outraged owner rescued it.

Just then, a farmer was jogging along the road behind a half-dozing horse. Lad's painful nip on the horse's hind leg turned its drowsy jog into an attempted escape. Then, as the wagon rolled past him, Lad leaped upward, skillfully caught a corner of the farmer's lap robe, and hauled it free of the seat. Robe in mouth, the collie pranced off into a field. Then, playfully keeping just out of reach of the pursuing farmer, he tossed the stolen treasure in a bramble patch far from the road.

Next, Lad made his way back to The Place by way of a neighbor's grounds. This neighbor owned a mean-eyed pest of a dog that Lad usually didn't bother noticing. But he certainly noticed the dog now. He forced it out of its kennel and gave it a thrashing that brought its owner's entire family shrieking to the scene of the conflict. Faced with a half-dozen shouting humans, Lad thought it best to trot toward home.

Back at The Place, a large white object fluttered from a clothesline. It was clearly a nurse's uniform, clearly the nurse's uniform. And Lad was delighted to see it. In less than two seconds, the uniform was off the line and torn in three places. In less than thirty seconds, it was lying in the mud bordering the lake, and Lad was rolling on it.

Lad was delightedly, idiotically, criminally happy. And, for this one time in his life, he was acting like a fool.

All day long, complaints came pouring in to The Master. Lad had destroyed all the cream. Lad had chased the red cow till it would be a miracle if she didn't fall sick. Lad had scared poor little Peter Grimm so badly that the cat seemed likely to spend all the rest of its nine lives howling in the treetop. Lad had spoiled a Sunday leg of mutton. Lad had made a respectable horse run madly away, and made the horse's owner run across a plowed field to recover his precious, and now ruined lap robe. Lad had nearly killed a neighbor's dog. Lad had destroyed the nurse's newest uniform. All day it was Lad, Lad, Lad!

To each and every person who complained, The Master answered, "Leave him alone. Lad and I have just gotten out of hell! He's doing things I'd do myself if I had the nerve." Which, of course, was a totally silly way for a grown man to talk.

Long after dusk, Lad meekly came home, feeling very tired. His spell of foolishness had worn itself out. Now he was a little ashamed of his pranks, and wondered why he had behaved so. Still, he could not grieve over what he had done. He could not grieve over anything just yet. The Mistress was alive!

Tired, but at peace with the world, Lad curled up under the piano and went to sleep. He slept so soundly that the locking of the house for the night did not awaken him. But something else did—something that occurred long after everyone was sound asleep.

Lad was eagerly chasing a whole army of squirrels through dreamland when, in a moment, he was wide awake and on guard. Far off, he heard a man walking. Someone had climbed the fence and was crossing the grounds toward the house. It was a man, and he was still nearly two hundred yards away. Moreover, he was walking sneakily, and stopping every now and then as if to listen. No human, at that distance, could have heard the steps. No dog could have avoided hearing them.

A trumpeting bark of warning sprang into Lad's throat. But the sharp command "Quiet!" was still in force. Even in his madness that day, Lad had uttered no sound. So Lad strangled back the excited bark. Instead, he listened in silence. He rose to his feet and came out from under the piano. He stood in the middle of the living room, head lowered, ears pricked. His ruff was bristling. His lips had slipped back from his teeth. And so he stood and waited.

The shuffling steps were nearer now. Down through the trees they came, and then onto The Lawn. Now they crunched lightly on the gravel of the drive. Lad moved forward a little, and again stood at attention.

The man was climbing onto the veranda. Then his footsteps sounded lightly on the veranda itself. Next there was a faint clicking noise at the lock of one of the bay windows. Slowly, the window began to rise.

There was another pause, followed by the very faintest scratching. Searching for the catch, the intruder was running a knife blade along the crack of the inner wooden blinds. The blinds parted slowly. The man threw a leg over the windowsill. Then he stepped noiselessly into the room. He stood there a second, listening. But before he could stir or breathe, something in the darkness hurled itself upon him.

Without so much as a growl of warning, eighty pounds of muscular energy hit the intruder full in the chest. A set of hot-breathing jaws flashed, aiming for the man's jugular vein, but missing it by a half inch. In a fraction of a moment, the murderously snapping jaws sank into the thief's shoulder. Although collies usually snarl and growl while fighting, Lad attacked in total silence.

The thief was less considerate about letting The Mistress rest quietly. With a terrible screech, he reeled back, lost his balance, and crashed to the floor, overturning a table and a lamp in his fall.

The thief had thought it would be a good time to break into the house. He'd heard that all the dogs on The Place had been sent away because of The Mistress's illness. So he was certain that now he was being attacked, not by a dog, but by a devil. Fearing for his life, the burglar panicked. Yelling in terror, he frantically tried to push away his attacker. But when his clammy hand met a mass of thick, warm fur, the man's superstitious terror died. He knew he had awakened the house. But if he could rid himself of this silent, terrible creature, he thought he still had time to escape. So he staggered to his feet and stabbed at Lad with his knife.

Because Lad was a collie, he avoided being killed then and there. Unlike some breeds that hang onto their holds until their deaths, collies can quickly shift holds. Collies, like wolves, can bite or slash a dozen times in a dozen different parts of the body. They are not pleasant opponents. So as the man lunged at Lad's chest, the dog let go of the shoulder hold. The knife blade plowed an ugly groove along the collie's side, but missed his heart.

Rapidly shifting holds, Lad's fangs then slashed the man's arm from elbow to wrist, clean through to the bone. The knife clattered to the floor. The thief wheeled and made a leap for the open window. He had not cleared half the space when Lad bounded for the back of the thief's neck. The dog's teeth raked the man's skull, carrying away a handful of hair and flesh. His weight threw the thief forward.

Twisting, the man found the dog's furry throat. As he backed out through the window, the burglar tried to strangle the dog with both hands. But it is not easy to strangle a collie. The piles of ruff hair form a protection no other breed of dog can boast. Scarcely had the hands found their grip when one of them was crushed between the dog's vise-like jaws.

Landing on the veranda, the thief finally threw off his enemy. But before he could turn and run away, Lad was at his throat again. The two crashed down onto the driveway below.

Carrying a pistol and flashlight, The Master ran down to find the living room strewn with blood and smashed furniture. As he flashed his light through the opened window, he saw the intruder sprawled, senseless, on his back.

Above him was Lad. The great dog was steadily grinding his way through toward the man's jugular.

There was a great deal of noise and excitement after that. The thief was tied up, and the local police were called. Everybody seemed to be talking loudly. Lad took advantage of the confusion to slip back into the house and to his cave under the piano. There he began to tenderly lick the flesh wound on his left side.

Lad was very tired. But more than that, he was very worried and unhappy. For in spite of all his own attempts at silence, the thief had made a tremendous amount of noise. The commandment "Quiet!" had been broken. And, somehow, Lad felt to blame. Would The Master punish him? Perhaps. Humans have such odd ideas of justice.

Finally The Master found Lad, and called him out from his hiding place. Head drooping, tail low, the collie crept out to meet his scolding. He looked just like a puppy caught tearing up a new rug. Then suddenly, The Master and everyone else in the room started patting him and telling him how wonderful he was. The Master found the deep scratch on his side and was tending it, and praising him again. And then, as a crowning reward, Lad was taken upstairs for The Mistress to pet and make a fuss over.

When at last he was sent downstairs again, Lad did not return to his cave under the piano. Instead, he went outdoors and away from The Place. When he thought he was far enough from the house, he sat down and began to bark.

It felt wonderful to be able to bark again. He'd had two weeks' worth of barks in his system, pushing to get out. So for the next half-hour, with a thunderous noise, Lad let them all come out. Then, feeling much better, he walked homeward, to take up normal life again.

CHAPTER 3

A Miracle or Two

There was only one creature in the entire world that Lad allowed to bully him. That was his mate, Lady. Lad and Lady were as odd a couple as one could find throughout northern New Jersey. Lady was high strung and flighty, and often teased Lad. Lad allowed Lady to do things that would have brought any other dog painfully close to death.

Sometimes human guests came to The Place. These guests were often people who were either frightened of dogs, or else insisted on mauling them. Lad hated guests. But he knew The Law far too well to snap or growl at them.

One cold spring morning, a guest came to The Place. Or maybe there were two guests? Lad wasn't sure. He could see a woman. But in her arms she carried a bundle that might have been anything at all. Although the bundle was long, it was ridiculously light. Or, rather, pitifully light. For it contained a five-year-old child—a child who ought to have weighed more than forty pounds. But this one weighed barely twenty. The child had a shriveled little face, and a body that was powerless from the waist down.

Six months earlier, the child had been as strong and happy as a collie pup. Until an invisible Something prowled through the land, laying its fingertips on thousands of happy and healthy youngsters, with a terrible effect. This particular child had not died, as had so many others. At least, her brain and the upper half of her body had not died. Her mother was advised to try mountain air for the hopeless little child. So she wrote to her distant relative, The Mistress, asking permission to spend a month at The Place.

Lad viewed the arrival of the adult guest with no interest, and with even less pleasure. He stood aloof, as the newcomer got out of the car. But, when The Master took the bundle from her arms and carried it up the steps, Lad became curious. Not only because The Master handled his burden so carefully, but also because the collie's sense of smell told him that it was human. Lad had never seen a human carried like this. It did not make sense to him. So he stepped forward to investigate.

The Master laid the bundle tenderly on the veranda hammock swing and loosened the blanket that was wrapped around it. Lad came over and looked down into the pitiful little face.

There had been no child at The Place for many years. Lad had seldom seen one up close. But now the sight did something strange to his heart—the big heart that always went out to the weak and defenseless. Lad sniffed in friendly fashion at the child's face.

When the child saw Lad, a look of pleased interest came into her dull eyes. Two weak little hands reached out and buried themselves lovingly in the fur that circled Lad's neck. The dog quivered with joy at the touch. He laid his great head down beside the pale cheek. He delighted in the pain that The Child's tugging fingers inflicted on his sensitive throat.

The Child's mother came up the steps after The Master. Seeing the huge dog, she halted in alarm. "Look out!" she cried. "He may attack her! Oh, please drive him away!"

"Who?" asked The Mistress. "Lad? Why, Lad wouldn't harm a hair of her head! See, he adores her already. I never knew him to take to a stranger before. And she looks happier than she has in months. Don't make her cry by sending him away."

"But," insisted the woman, "dogs are full of germs. He might give her something terrible."

"Lad is just as clean as I am," declared The Mistress. "There isn't a day he doesn't swim in the lake, and there isn't a day I don't brush him. He's—"

"He's a collie, though," protested the guest, while her daughter grabbed onto the delighted dog's ruff. "And I've always heard collies are untrustworthy. Don't you find them so?"

"If we did," said The Master, "we wouldn't keep them. I'll call him away, though, if it bothers you to have him so close to your girl. Come, Lad!"

Reluctantly, the dog turned to obey The Law. But as he went, he looked back at the adorable new friend he had made. Then he crossed obediently to where The Master stood.

The Child's face puckered unhappily. Her thin arms went out toward the collie. In a tired little voice she called after him, "Doggie! Come back here, right away! I love you, Dog!"

Lad eagerly glanced up at The Master for permission to answer the call. The Master, in turn, looked questioningly at his nervous guest. Lad translated the look. Instantly, he felt hatred for the fussy woman.

The guest walked over to her daughter and explained, "Dogs aren't nice pets for sick little girls, dear. They're rough. And besides, they bite. I'll find Dolly for you as soon as I unpack."

"I don't want Dolly!" cried The Child. "I want the dog! He isn't rough. He won't bite. Doggie! I love you! Come here!"

Lad looked up longingly at The Master, his tail wagging, his eyes dancing. With one hand, The Master motioned toward the hammock. Lad did not wait for a second invitation. Quietly he crossed behind the guest, and stood beside his new friend. The Child squealed with delight, and drew his head down to her face.

"Oh, well!" the guest surrendered. "If she won't be happy any other way, let him go to her. I suppose it's safe, if you say so. And it's the first thing she's been interested in since—" She broke off. Then she said sternly, "No, darling. You must not kiss him! I draw the line at that. Here. Let Mamma wipe off your lips with her handkerchief."

"Dogs aren't made to be kissed," said The Master. "But kissing the head of a clean dog is safer than kissing the mouths of most humans. I'm glad she likes Lad. And I'm even gladder that he likes her. He almost never approaches outsiders of his own free will."

That was how Lad's new friendship began.

And that, too, was how a sick child found a new interest in life.

Every day, Lad was with The Child. Leaving his cave under the piano, he lay all night outside the door of her bedroom. Instead of romping in the forest with Lady, he strolled majestically beside The Child, as she rode in her wheelchair along the walkways, or up and down the veranda.

As the days went on, The Child enjoyed her shaggy playmate more than ever. To her, the dog was fascinating. She loved to make him "speak" or shake hands or lie down or stand up when she asked. She loved to play games with him, such as Beauty and the Beast, and the Fairy Princess and the Dragon.

Lad eagerly took on the roles of Beast and Dragon. Of course, he always played his part wrong. So in frustration, The Child always ended up hitting him with her weak fists. And Lad always accepted this punishment with a grin of happiness.

Whether due to the bracing mountain air or because of her friendship with Lad, The Child was growing stronger by the day. Relieved to see this steady improvement, her mother continued to tolerate Lad's friendship with her daughter. However, she never lost her own fear of the dog.

Two or three things happened to revive this foolish dread. One of them occurred about a week after the guests' arrival at The Place. Since Lady was no fonder of guests than was Lad, she had stayed away from them. But one day, as The Child lay in the hammock trying to teach Lad the alphabet, Lady trotted around the corner of the porch. Seeing The Child, Lady paused and stood still, blinking curiously.

The Child spied the graceful gold and white creature. Pushing Lad to one side, she called, "Come here, new Doggie. You pretty, pretty Doggie!"

Flattered by The Child's words, Lady strolled forward. When she came within arm's reach, she halted again. The Child thrust out one hand, and suddenly grabbed her by the ruff to draw her into petting distance.

The little tug on Lady's fur was nothing compared to the maulings that Lad endured. But Lad and Lady were very different. Lady did not share Lad's endless patience and love for the weak. At the first pinch of her sensitive skin, Lady bared her teeth and slashed at the thin little arm that tried to pull her closer.

At the same moment, Lad hurled himself between his mate and his friend. It was an unbelievably swift move for so large a dog. And it served its purpose. Instead of cutting the little girl's arm, Lady's slash sent a red groove of blood along Lad's shoulder. Before Lady could snap again, Lad used his shoulder to ease her off the edge of the veranda steps. He did this very gently, but he did it firmly.

In angry amazement at such rudeness on the part of her mate, Lady snarled and bit at him. Just then, The Child's mother came rushing to her child's rescue. The noise also brought The Master running to the veranda.

"He growled at my daughter," the mother reported hysterically. "He growled at her, and then he and that other horrid brute got to fighting, and—"

"Pardon me," interrupted The Master, calling both dogs to him, "No male dog would fight with Lady. And certainly not Lad—"

"Hey!" The Master broke off. "Look at his shoulder! That cut was meant for your child. Instead of scolding Lad, you should thank him for saving her from an ugly slash. I'll keep Lady chained up, after this."

"But—"

"With Lad beside her, the child is in about as much danger as if she were being guarded by forty Marines," The Master continued. "Take my word for it."

Then, turning to his dogs, The Master said, "Come along, Lady. It's the kennel for you for the next few weeks, old girl. Lad, when I get back, I'll wash that shoulder for you."

With a sigh, Lad went over to the hammock and lay down. For the first time since The Child's arrival, he was unhappy—very unhappy. He'd had to shove and fend off Lady, whom he worshipped. And he knew it would be a long time before his mate would forgive or forget. And all because he had saved a child from injury—a child who had meant no harm and who could not help herself! All at once, life seemed sadly complex to Lad's simple soul.

Lad whimpered a little, and lifted his head toward the little girl's hand, hoping for a caress to make things easier. But the little girl had been very displeased at Lady's reaction to her friendly advances. She couldn't punish Lady for this. But she could punish Lad.

The Child slapped Lad's muzzle with all her might. For once, Lad was not amused by the punishment. He sighed, and curled up on the floor beside the hammock. His head was between his forepaws. His great sorrowful eyes were full of bewildered grief.

Spring drowsed into early summer. And with the passing days, The Child continued to look less and less like a mummy, and more like a thin, but normal, girl of five. She ate and slept as she had not done for many months. The lower half of her body still seemed lifeless. But there was a faint glow of pink in her cheeks, and her eyes were alive once more.

One hot morning in early June, when The Mistress and The Master had driven over to the village for the mail, The Child's mother wheeled her daughter to a shady nook down by the lake. It was just the spot a city dweller would have chosen for a nap. It was also just the spot a country person would have avoided. For here, the ground was seldom dry. Here the grass grew thickest. Here lived frogs and lizards. And here poisonous snakes could come out from their hiding places in the stone crannies of the lake wall to enjoy the coolness and moisture of the long grass. Here, in fact, not three days earlier, The Master had killed a copperhead snake.

If either The Mistress or The Master had been at home, the guest would have been warned against taking her daughter there. She would have been doubly warned against lifting The Child from the wheelchair, and placing her on a rug in the grass. But here, on its mattress of lush grasses, the rug was soft. The lake breeze stirred the branches of the willows. The air was cool, and had lost the dead hotness that hung over the higher ground. The guest was very pleased with her choice of a resting place.

Lad was not.

The big dog had been growing uneasy from the time the wheelchair approached the lake wall. Twice he put himself in front of it, only to be ordered aside. As The Child was laid upon her grassy bed, Lad barked loudly and pulled at one end of the rug. The guest shook her parasol at him and ordered him back to the house. But Lad obeyed no orders except those of The Master and The Mistress.

Instead of slinking away, Lad sat down beside The Child. He did not lie down as usual, but sat with his ears erect, dark eyes cloudy with trouble, nostrils pulsing. The dog was uneasy. His uneasiness would not let him sit still. It made him fidget and shift his position. Once or twice, he growled a little under his breath.

After a while, his eyes brightened, and his tail began to thud gently on the edge of the rug. He'd heard The Place's car turning in from the highway. In it were The Mistress and The Master, coming home with the mail. Now everything would be all right. For now Lad could let the humans take over guard duty.

As the car rounded the corner of the house and came to a stop at the front door, the guest caught sight of it. Jumping up from her seat on the rug, she started toward it, eager to get her mail. As she rose, she dislodged one of the wall's small stones and sent it rattling down into a wide crack between two larger rocks. She did not notice the tinkle of stone on stone. Nor did she hear the sharp little hiss that followed, as the falling stone struck a sleeping copperhead snake in one of the wall's lowest cavities. But Lad heard it. And he heard the slithering of scales against rock, as the snake angrily searched for new sleeping quarters.

Before the guest had walked more than a few steps away, a reddish head pushed out from the bottom of the wall. The copperhead then glided out of its hole onto the grass at the edge of the rug. The snake was short and thick and dirty, with a wedge-shaped head. Between eye and nostril was the sinister "pinhole," which is the mark of the poisonous serpent. The reptile oozed out from the wall and moved along the fringe of the rug. Then it paused, dazzled by the light. It stopped within a yard of The Child's little hand, which was resting on the rug. The little girl's other arm was around Lad. Her body was between him and the snake.

With a shiver, Lad freed himself from the weak embrace and got nervously to his feet.

There are two things that frighten a collie. One is a mad dog. The other is a poisonous snake. So at the sight of the copperhead, Lad's brave heart failed him. He had courageously attacked humans who'd invaded The Place. More than once, he had fearlessly fought with larger dogs. Usually, Lad knew no fear. Yet now he was afraid—trembling, sickly afraid. Afraid of the deadly thing that had stopped within three feet of him. The only barrier between him and danger was The Child's thin body.

By now, The Master had gotten out of the car and was coming down the hill with several letters in his hand. Lad cast a pleading look at him. But he knew The Master was too far away to be summoned in time by even the most commanding bark.

It was then that The Child's gaze fell on the snake. With a gasp, the little girl shrank back against Lad. The upper half of her body moved away from the danger. But her legs and feet lay motionless. The motion jerked the rug's fringe an inch or two, disturbing the copperhead. The snake coiled and drew back its three-cornered head, the fork-like tongue darting in and out.

With a cry of panic, The Child picked up a picture book from the rug beside her, and threw it at the snake. The book missed its mark. But it gave the copperhead reason to believe itself attacked. Back went the triangular head. And then it flashed forward.

But before the snake could bite her, The Child was knocked flat by a mighty, furry shape lunging across her toward her enemy. The copperhead's fangs sank deep in Lad's nose.

Giving no sign of pain, Lad sprang back. He caught The Child by the shoulder of her shirt. Without even bruising her soft flesh, he half-dragged, half-threw her into the grass behind him. Then Lad threw himself upon the coiled snake. As the collie charged, the snake's swift-striking fangs found a second mark, this time in the side of Lad's jaw.

An instant later, the copperhead lay twisting among the weeds. Its back was broken, and its body cut almost in two by a slash of the dog's teeth. The fight was over. The danger was past. The Child was safe. But now, in her rescuer's muzzle and jaw, there were two deposits of deadly poison.

Lad stood panting above the crying child. His work was done. Instinct told him how much that work had cost him. But The Child he worshipped was unhurt, so the collie was happy. Lad bent down to lick the upset little face as a silent plea to be pardoned for having had to be rough with her. But he was denied even this tiny consolation. For as he leaned downward, Lad was knocked flat by a blow that all but fractured his skull.

At The Child's first terrified cry, her mother turned back—but not in time to notice the snake. The first thing she'd seen was the dog knocking flat her sick child. Then she watched it grip the child by the shoulder with its teeth, and drag her, shrieking, along the ground. That was enough. The mother's protective instinct was aroused. Fearless of danger to herself, the guest rushed to her child's rescue. As she ran, she swung her parasol overhead.

Down came the parasol's heavy metal handle. It struck Lad's head with a force that knocked him to the ground. As Lad staggered to his feet, the makeshift weapon arose once more. This time it landed on his broad shoulders.

Lad did not try to dodge or run. He did not show his teeth. Because his mad attacker was a woman, he would not fight back. And because she was a guest, the Guest Law made her sacred. Lad's head and shoulders quivered under the pain of the blows. And the woman, wild with fear and love for her child, continued to hit with all her strength.

Then came the rescue. As soon as she saw her mother hit Lad, The Child cried out in protest. "Mother!" she shrieked. "Mother! Don't! Don't! He kept the snake from eating me! He—!"

But her cry went unheard. The woman, too frantic to listen, kept beating the dog.

The Child felt the pain of each blow in her own tender heart. Finally, she made a wild and desperate move to protect her beloved playmate. Scrambling to her feet, The Child stumbled forward three steps, and seized her mother by the skirt.

The woman looked down. Then her face went white, and the parasol clattered to the ground. For an instant the mother stood frozen—her eyes wide and glazed, her mouth open, her cheeks ashy. She stared at her daughter, who now stood unsteadily on her feet, swaying and clutching the dress for support, begging her not to hurt Lad.

Seeing his dog being beaten, The Master, furious, had broken into a run. Now he came to a sudden halt. He, too, stared dazedly at the miracle before him.

The Child had risen and had walked. The Child had walked! She, whom the wise doctors had declared paralyzed, with no hope of ever walking again!

Small wonder that both guest and Master stood amazed. And yet as a team of doctors later agreed, there was no miracle, no magic about it. The Child was not the first, nor the last case, in which paralyzed limbs had been restored by means of a shock.

The Child had had no birth defect or spinal injury that would cause paralysis. It was a long illness that left her powerless. Country air and a new interest in life had gradually built up wasted tissues. A shock had re-established communication between her brain and lower body.

Finally, The Master found the copperhead's torn body. And the mother listened to her child. "I'll get down on my knees to that heaven-sent dog," sobbed the guest. "I must apologize to him. Where is he?"

There was no answer. Lad had vanished. Nor did he come when called.

The Master made a search through the forest. But he did not find Lad. Finally, The Master asked The Child to tell her story all over again. Then he nodded. "I understand," he said, holding back tears. "The snake must have bitten him. And probably more than once. Lad would have known what that meant. For Lad knows everything—I mean, knew everything."

The Master paused, and then continued sorrowfully, "If Lad had known a little less, he'd have been human. But if he'd been human, he probably wouldn't have thrown away his life for a child."

"Thrown away his life?" repeated the guest.

"I don't understand. Surely I didn't strike him hard enough to—"

"No," replied The Master. "You didn't. But the snake did."

"You mean—?"

"I mean, it is the nature of all animals to crawl away, so they can die alone. They don't want to cause any further trouble to those they have loved. Lad knew he'd gotten his death from the copperhead's fangs. So while we stared in wonder at The Child's cure, Lad quietly went away to die."

The guest dissolved into a flood of tears. "And I beat him!" she wailed. "I beat him horribly! And all the time he was dying from the poison he'd saved my child from getting. Oh, I'll never forgive myself for this—not as long as I live!"

"Most humans learn to forgive themselves," The Master commented coldly. "Lad was only a dog, after all. That's why he is dead."

When The Mistress heard about Lad, she was grief-stricken. For she loved the great dog more than she loved most humans.

The Place tingled with joy over The Child's cure. Her uncertain, but always successful, efforts at walking were a delight. But through the joy, The Mistress and The Master could not always keep their faces bright. Even the guest mourned Lad's passing. And the little girl was heartbroken at the loss of her friend.

At dawn on the morning of the fourth day, The Master let himself silently out of the house. He set out on his usual cross-country walk. For years, Lad had been his companion on these early morning walks. Now, with a heavy heart, The Master prepared to set out alone. As the door shut behind him, The Master noticed something stiffly get up from the porch rug. The Master stared in dazed disbelief.

The Something was a dog. Yet no such dog had ever before dirtied The Place's well-scrubbed veranda. The animal's body was lean to the point of starvation. Its head was badly swollen, though the swelling seemed to be going down. The fur was one solid mass of caked mud.

The Master sat down very suddenly on the veranda floor beside the dirt-encrusted animal. Catching it in his arms, he sputtered, "Lad! Laddie! Old friend! You're alive! You're—you're—alive!"

Yes, Lad had known enough to creep away to the woods to die. But thanks to the wolf strain in his collie blood, he had also known how to do something far wiser than die. His natural instincts had taught him how to survive a snakebite. He had buried himself up to the nostrils in the muddy marsh behind the forest. The swamp's mysteriously healing ooze drew out the snake venom. After three days, the mud bath left him whole again. Lad was thin and shaky, and his head still swollen. But he was whole.

The Master's joyous shout brought the whole family running to the veranda.

"But don't you think he's awfully dirty?" the guest commented, keeping her distance. "Awfully dirty and—"

"Yes," The Master snapped back, cradling Lad's muddy head in his loving hands. "Awfully dirty. That's why he's still alive."

CHAPTER 4

His Little Son

After defeating Knave, Lad was happy having his mate all to himself. Together he and Lady roamed the forests beyond The Place in search of rabbits. Together they sprawled on the old fur rug in front of the fireplace. Together they worshipped The Mistress and The Master.

Then, in the late summer, a new rival—or rather, three rivals—appeared. They took up all of Lady's time and love. And poor Lad was made to feel left out in the cold. The trio of rivals were fuzzy, and about the size of month-old kittens. In short, they were three collie puppies.

When they were barely two weeks old, two of the puppies died. There seemed to be no reason for their deaths. It's simply the nature of the breed. Only a fuzzy grayish baby was left, a puppy that was soon to turn to white and gold. The Mistress named him "Wolf."

The mother dog gave Baby Wolf all of her attention, which made Lad very lonely. The great collie would try to lure his mate into a romp on The Lawn. But Lady either ignored him or gave him a snarl. In fact, when Lad came too near the fuzzy baby, the mother warned him off, either with an angry growl or a slash of her teeth.

Lad did not understand the instinctive mother's love that kept Lady with Wolf all day and all night. He felt only a mildly disapproving curiosity about the little ball of fur that nestled against his beloved mate's side.

After a week or two of trying to win back Lady's interest, Lad gave up. He took long walks by himself in the forest, brooded for hours in his favorite cave under the piano, and tried to cheer himself up by spending all the rest of his day with The Mistress and The Master. And he came to completely disapprove of Wolf.

The puppy was beginning to emerge from his newborn shapelessness. His blunt little nose was growing thin and pointed. His butterball body was growing longer. He looked more like a dog now, and less like a walking muff.

Wolf was also becoming playful. He found Lady to be a pleasant playmate, up to a point. But sometimes Wolf's clownish roughness got on her tense nerves. When Lady thought his games had gone far enough, she stopped them with a breathtaking slap of one of her forepaws. So the frisky puppy turned to Lad in search of another playmate, only to find that Lad would not play with him at all. Lad made it very clear to everyone except the foolish puppy that he wanted nothing to do with him. But he did not snap or growl when the puppy teased. He simply walked away.

Wolf had a genius for tormenting Lad. For instance, while the huge collie was snoozing away on the veranda or under the wisteria vines, Wolf would pounce upon him from out of nowhere. The puppy would grab his sleeping father by the ear, and drive his sharp little teeth fiercely into the flesh. Then he would pull backward, with the idea of dragging Lad along the ground. Lad would wake in pain, unhappily get to his feet, and start to walk off, with the puppy still hanging onto his ear. But since Wolf was a collie and not a bulldog, the puppy would lose his grip as soon as his fat little body left the ground.

Then Wolf would pursue Lad, throwing himself against his father's forelegs and nipping his ankles. All this was torture to the great collie, and embarrassing, too—especially if humans happened to witness the scene. It was bad enough that Wolf had taken his place in Lady's heart, without also humiliating him in the eyes of his gods! Yet Lad never struck back. He simply got out of the way.

So Lad moped, and started leaving half his dinner uneaten. Lady remained nervously fussy over her one child. And Wolf continued to be a lovable pest.

Then one November morning, Lady met Wolf's playfulness with a yell of rage so savage that the puppy scampered away in terror. The Master came running out from his study. He knew no normal dog gives that terrible a yell except when in great pain or in illness.

The Master called Lady over to him. She obeyed, slinking up to him unwillingly. Her nose was hot and dry; her soft brown eyes were glazed.

After examining her, The Master shut her into a kennel room and telephoned a veterinarian.

"She has distemper," reported the vet an hour later. "Dogs rarely get distemper after they're a year old. But when they do, it's dangerous—and highly contagious. Better let me take her over to my hospital and isolate her there. I may be able to cure her in a month or two, or I may not. Anyhow, there's no use in risking your other dogs' lives by leaving her here."

So it was that Lad saw his dear mate taken away from him in the back seat of a stranger's car. Lady hated to go. She whimpered as the vet lifted her aboard. At the sound of her whimper, Lad started forward, growling. At a sharp word of command from The Master, Lad stopped and stood, confused. He looked at Lady, his dark eyes filled with sorrow, then glanced at The Master pleadingly.

"It's all right, Laddie," said The Master, stroking the dog's head as he spoke. "It's all right. It's the only chance of saving her."

Lad did not understand the words, but their tone was reassuring. It told him that this kidnapping was legal and must not be prevented. Sadly, he watched the car chug out of sight, up the drive. Then, with a sigh, he walked back to his cave beneath the piano.

The next morning, as soon as the doors were opened, Lad dashed out in search of Lady. With some faint hope that she might have been brought back in the night, he searched every corner of The Place for her.

Lad did not find Lady. But Wolf very quickly found Lad. Wolf was lonely, too—very lonely. He had just spent the first night alone of his three-month life. He missed the furry, warm body he had always cuddled against when he slept. He missed the pretty mother who had been his companion.

The eyes of even happy collie pups have a mournful look. This morning, loneliness intensified the sad expression in Wolf's eyes. But at the sight of Lad, the puppy romped forward with a bark of joy. The world was not quite empty, after all. Though his mother had gone away, at least here was a playmate. It was better than nothing. The little pup frisked up to Lad.

Lad saw him coming. The older dog halted and turned away to avoid the lively little nuisance. Then, halfway around, he stopped and turned back to face the puppy.

Lady was gone, maybe forever. And all that was left to remind Lad of her was this troublesome little son of hers. Lady had loved this youngster—Lady, whom Lad so loved. Only Wolf was left, and Wolf was in some mysterious way a part of Lady. So, instead of escaping as the pest trotted toward him, Lad stood where he was.

Wolf jumped up and nipped merrily at one of Lad's ears. Lad did not shake off his tormentor and stalk away as usual. In spite of the pain, he remained quiet, looking down at the puppy with a sort of sorrowful friendliness. Lad seemed to realize that Wolf, too, was lonely. And the little dog was helpless, as well.

Tired of biting Lad's ear, Wolf dived for his

father's forelegs and gnawed happily at them. Lad endured this new bother without flinching.

After a while, Wolf stopped this play. Lad crossed to the veranda and lay down. The puppy trotted over to him and stood for a moment, ears cocked and head on one side, as if planning a new attack on his victim. Then, with a little satisfied whimper, he curled up close against his father's shaggy side and went to sleep.

Confused, Lad gazed down at the sleeping puppy. He really didn't like being used as a pillow. But then, noticing some rumpled fur on the top of the puppy's sleepy head, he bent over and began softly licking it back into shape. The puppy mumbled drowsily in his sleep, and nestled more snugly against his new protector. And in this way, Lad became the guardian of his frisky little son.

Lad took his new duties very seriously. He not only put up with Wolf's teasing, but he also took charge of the puppy's education.

A puppy needs a great deal of educating. It is a job that tries the teacher's patience. Small wonder that many humans lose their temper during the process and foolishly resort to the use of force. In these cases, the puppy is never properly educated. Instead, he emerges from the process with a broken spirit, or a streak of meanness that makes him worthless. Time, patience, firmness, wisdom, self-control, and gentleness—these are the six absolute essentials for training a puppy. It is a rare human who is blessed with even three of these qualities. But since Lad was a dog, he possessed all six. And he needed them.

To begin with, Wolf loved to tear up or bury anything that could be torn or buried. A dropped handkerchief, a cushion left on the grass, a book or a hat lying on a chair—-he looked on these as treasures, to be destroyed as quickly as possible. He also enjoyed taking a flying leap onto anyone asleep in the hammock. He howled nearly every night at the moon. If the night were moonless, he howled just for the fun of it.

He delighted at a chance to terrify the chickens or peacocks or any of the other creatures on The Place. He tried this form of bullying only once on The Mistress's gray cat, Peter Grimm. For the rest of the day, Wolf nursed a scratched nose and a torn ear. This adventure taught him to keep away from cats.

In addition, Wolf had a craving to find out whether or not things were good to eat. He experimented with everything, from clothespins to cigars. The climax came when he found a two-pound box of chocolates on the veranda table. Wolf ate not only all the candy inside, but the box, as well. After this, he was violently ill.

These were only a few of his happy sins.

Respectable, middle-aged Lad faced the burden of making Wolf into a decent canine citizen. It was a long, slow process. But Lad went at it with energy and patience. Once, for instance, Wolf leaped upon a lace handkerchief that had just fallen from The Mistress's belt. Before the sharp little teeth could rip the fine fabric into shreds, the amazed puppy found himself lifted gently by the scruff of his neck and held in midair until he dropped the handkerchief.

Lad then placed him on the grass. Wolf immediately pounced again upon the handkerchief. Once again he was lifted off the ground. After this was repeated five times, a gleam of understanding entered the puppy's fuzzy brain. He trotted grumpily away, leaving the handkerchief untouched.

Once when Wolf made a wild rush at the peacock chicks, Lad darted in between the pup and the chicks. Wolf was bowled over by the force of the impact. He lay for a minute on his back, the breath knocked out of his body.

It was easier to teach Wolf the rules about barking at people. With a sharp growl, Lad silenced the puppy's barking when a guest or tradesman entered The Place. With a threatening bark, Lad taught Wolf to bark loudly to scare away peddlers or tramps who tried to sneak toward the house.

It would take many pages to tell the full story of Wolf's education. Sometimes The Mistress and The Master, though amazed at Lad's patience, would doubt his success. Yet bit by bit, and in a surprisingly short time, Wolf's character was rounded into shape. But his education wasn't always a chore. Lad varied it by sometimes taking the puppy for long runs in the surrounding woods. Sometimes he relaxed by just playing with the little dog.

Wolf grew to love his father as he had never loved Lady. For Lad's consistent discipline and firm kindliness had a powerful effect on his heart, as well as on his manners. They struck a far deeper note within him than Lady's alternating love and crossness ever had. In fact, Wolf seemed to have forgotten Lady.

But Lad had not. Every morning, the moment he was let out of the house, Lad would trot over to Lady's empty kennel to see if she had come back to him during the night. There was eager hope in his big dark eyes as he hurried over to the vacant kennel. There was sorrow as he turned away from his hopeless quest.

Gray late autumn turned overnight into white early winter. The ground of The Place lay blanketed in snow. The lake at the foot of The Lawn was frozen solid from shore to shore.

The puppy loved the snow. He would roll in it and bite it, barking excitedly. His coat was thicker and shaggier now, to ward off the stinging cold. And the snow and the roaring winds were his playmates, rather than his enemies. Most of all, the frozen lake fascinated him. Earlier, when Lad had taught him to swim, Wolf had at first shrunk back from the chilly black water. Now, to his surprise, he could run on that water almost as easily as on land. It was a miracle he never tired of testing. He spent half his time on the ice, despite an occasional hard tumble or slide.

Once, and only once, had Lad discovered anything to remind him of his lost mate. And that discovery caused him to break the most sacred of The Place's simple Laws: the Guest Law.

One day in late November, a car came down the drive to the front door of the house. The vet who had taken Lady away was stopping by The Place to tell The Master about Lady's progress at his dog hospital. Lad was in the living room when a maid answered the door. The collie walked forward to welcome the guest, whom he had not yet seen. And as the vet stepped into the room by one door, The Master entered it from another—which was lucky for the vet.

Lad took one look at the man who had stolen Lady. Then, without warning, he threw himself straight at the vet's throat. Although the vet was used to the ways of dogs, he barely had time to throw one arm in front of his throat. Then, eighty pounds of collie hit him on the chest. Lad's powerful jaws closed on the forearm guarding his throat, and white teeth tore their way through his thick coat sleeve, clear through to the flesh.

"Lad!" shouted The Master, springing forward.

In obedience to the sharp command, Lad loosened his grip and dropped to the floor, where he stood quivering with fury. Through the rage that clouded his brain, Lad knew he had broken The Law. He had never before deserved punishment. And he wasn't afraid of it. But The Master's tone of fierce disapproval cut the dog's soul more painfully than any whip could have cut his body.

"Lad!" shouted The Master again, in amazement.

The dog turned, walked slowly over to The Master, and lay down at his feet. The Master, without another word, opened the front door and pointed outward. Lad rose and slunk out. He had been ordered from the house, and in a stranger's presence!

"He thinks I'm responsible for his losing Lady," said the vet. "That's why he went for me. I don't blame the dog. Don't beat him."

"I'm not going to beat him," growled The Master. "Besides, I've just punished him worse than if I'd taken an ax handle to him. Send me a bill for your coat."

In late December, a sudden thaw changed the white ground to mud, and turned the smooth surface of the lake ice to slush. It was the traditional January thaw, but it came early that year.

On the third and last morning of the thaw, Wolf galloped down to the lake, as usual. Lad jogged along at his side. As they reached the edge, Lad sniffed and drew back. A special sixth sense somehow told him that there was danger ahead. Wolf, however, was too young to heed such warnings. Right away, he frisked out upon the ice. A rough growl of warning from Lad made Wolf look back. But the lure of the ice was stronger than the call of duty.

For a few yards out, the rotting ice was still thick. But then, under the ice, the current twisted sharply toward land in a half-circle. And where the current ran, the ice was thin, and as soggy as wet paper. Wolf bounded onto the thinner ice, driving his hind claws into the slushy surface as he took a second leap. He was dismayed to find that the ice collapsed under his feet. There was a dull, sloppy sound. A ten-foot ice cake broke off from the main sheet, and immediately turned into a dozen smaller pieces. Suddenly Wolf disappeared, down into the swift-running water.

Then he came back to the surface at the outer edge of the hole. Furious at the trick his lake had played on him, Wolf struck out for shore. But his forefeet clawed helplessly at the ledge of ice. He was neither strong enough nor smart enough to succeed in crawling onto it in order make his way to land. The bitter chill of the water was already paralyzing him. The strong current was tugging at his hindquarters. Wolf began to panic and howl.

As The Mistress and The Master drove into the driveway from the road, they heard the noise. The lake was plainly visible to them through the bare trees, even at that distance. They jumped out of the car and set off at a run to the water's edge. But the lake was far away, and the ground was heavy with mud. They knew they'd never reach the lake before the puppy's strength would fail.

But Lad was already there. At Wolf's first cry, Lad sprang out onto the ice. His rush carried him to the edge of the hole. There, leaning forward and bracing all four of his paws, he tried to catch the puppy by the neck and lift him to safety. But before his rescuing jaws could close on Wolf's fur, the ice gave way beneath his weight, making the ten-foot hole twenty feet wider. As Lad went down with a crash, the piece of ice that had been supporting Wolf broke apart. Losing his foothold, the puppy sank into the icy water. Wolf strangled and splashed in terror, his mouth and throat so full of water he couldn't even howl.

Lad came to the surface a few feet away from where Wolf thrashed among the chunks of drifting ice. He swam out toward Wolf, butting aside the ice chunks with his great shoulders. His jaws gripped Wolf by the back, and he swam with him toward shore. At the edge of the ice ledge, Lad gave a mighty heave, flinging Wolf's body halfway onto the solid surface. The puppy's flying forepaws struck the ice. His sharp claws bit into its upper crust. With a frantic wriggle, he was out of the water and on top of this thicker section of ice. In a second, he reached the shore and was racing wildly up The Lawn toward the safety of his kennel.

Halfway up the hill, courage returned to the soaking wet puppy. He halted, turned around, and barked, challenging the water to come ashore and fight fair.

But as Wolf's forepaws had gripped the ice, the puppy had also pushed downward with his hind legs. Both his hind paws had struck Lad's head and driven him completely under water. There, the great collie was caught by the current. When Lad came up, it was not to the surface, but under the ice. The top of his head struck against the underside of the ice sheet.

A lesser dog would have thrashed about uselessly until he drowned. Maybe by instinct, maybe by reason, Lad headed toward the light. This was the spot where the great hole let in sunshine through the gray ice sheet. He fought his way on against the current, beneath the ice, always toward the light. And just as his lungs were ready to burst, Lad reached the open space.

Sputtering and panting, Lad headed for shore. Soon he arrived at the ice ledge that lay between him and the bank. He reached it just as The Master began to work his way out over the swaying ice toward him.

Twice the big dog raised himself almost to the top of the ledge. Once, the ice broke under his weight, drenching him. The second time, Lad got his forequarters well over the top of the ledge. He was struggling upward when The Master's hand gripped his soaked ruff. With this new help, Lad made one final struggle. This time he landed, gasping, but safe, on the slushy surface of the thicker ice. He and The

Master crawled backward over the few yards that still separated them from land.

Lad staggered forward to greet The Mistress. His eyes were still dim from his fearful ordeal. But halfway toward The Mistress, his path was barred by a dog—one that suddenly fell upon him with ecstatic delight. Lad cleared his waterlogged nostrils in a growl of protest. He was in no mood to have Wolf rob him of The Mistress's attention. Surely he had already done enough for Wolf today. Tired and dizzy, all he wanted was the petting and praise that only The Mistress could give.

Finally, impatience at the puppy cleared the haze from Lad's brain and eyes. He stopped and stared, dumbfounded. The dog that greeted him so delightedly was not Wolf. It was Lady! Oh, it was Lady!

"We've just brought her back to you, old friend," The Master was telling him. "We went over for her in the car this morning. She's well again, and—"

But Lad did not hear. All he knew, and all he wanted to know, was that his mate was happily nipping one of his ears to make him romp with her. It was a sharp nip, and it hurt very much. But after six long weeks, Lad loved the feel of that playful nip.

CHAPTER 5

For a Bit of Ribbon

A guest started all the trouble—a guest who loved dogs far better than he understood them.

"Say!" said the guest, at the end of his visit to The Place. "If I had a dog like Lad, I'd have him compete in dog shows. You know, there's going to be a big one next month at Madison Square Garden in New York. Why not take a chance and show him there? Think how proud you'd be if the big dog won a Westminster blue ribbon!"

The man meant well. And no harm might have come from his suggestion. But the next day, The Master noticed an announcement in the newspaper about the upcoming dog show. He asked The Mistress her opinion. And it was she who cast the deciding vote. "Lad is twice as beautiful as any collie we ever saw at the show," she declared. "And a blue ribbon is the greatest honor a dog can have. It would be something to remember."

After that, The Master wrote a letter to a friend, asking his advice.

The friend wrote back, "I don't pretend to know anything about collies, since Airedales are my specialty. But Lad is a beauty, and his pedigree shows that he comes from a long line of champions. I'd think it's worth the entrance fee, if I were you. And since I'm showing four of my Airedales there, we'll have a chance to see each other."

Then the friend suggested, "If you don't want to risk too much money, why not just enter him for the Novice Class? It's a competition for dogs that have never before been shown. If he wins as a Novice, you can enter him in something more important at a another time."

Encouraged, The Master filled out the application and sent it with the entrance fee. After a while, he received word that "Sunnybank Lad" was entered for the Novice Class, at the Westminster Kennel Club's annual show at Madison Square Garden.

By this time, both The Mistress and The Master had caught "show fever." They talked of little else than the upcoming show. They read all the dog show literature they could get their hands on. As for Lad, he was mercifully ignorant of what was in store for him.

The Mistress began to have an inkling of what Lad was in for when she read some of the Kennel Club's rules. For twelve hours a day, the dogs had to be on display for the judges and guests. For the entire four days of the show, the dogs had to stay at Madison Square Garden. "But Lad's never been away from home a night in his life!" exclaimed The Mistress. "He'll be horribly lonely there, especially at night."

By this time, Lad began to be aware that something unusual was going on. It made him restless. But he did not connect it with himself until The Mistress took to giving him daily baths and brushings. In the past, The Mistress always brushed him once a day, to keep his shaggy coat fluffy and glossy. Swimming in the lake made him as clean as any human. But Lad had never undergone such vigorous combing and brushing as he did now.

As a result of this grooming, his wavy fur was like spun silk. His white chest and forepaws were like snow. And his sides, broad back, and mighty shoulders shone like bronze. Lad was magnificent. But he was miserable. By now, he knew he was in some way the center of all this unwanted excitement. Like most dogs, Lad hated change of any sort. And this particular change seemed to threaten his peace.

All over the East, hundreds of purebred dogs were being prepared for this competition. To humans, the show is pure entertainment. To dogs, it is absolute torture. But since The Master and The Mistress had never before been to a dog show, they had no idea of this torture. If they had, all the blue ribbons ever woven would not have tempted them to subject their beloved pet to it.

But shows have traditions that must be followed, no matter how painful. For example, Airedales naturally have a beautiful, soft, gray outer coat. But judges traditionally award ribbons only to Airedales with no gray fur. So some people who show Airedales pluck out all the gray hairs, one by one—even though doing so hurts as much as pulling hairs from a human head. To make bull terriers' white coats even whiter, some owners rub harsh clay into their tender skin. To add to their "beauty" (as well as their pain), owners sometimes sandpaper the dogs' sensitive tails and ears. To prepare collies for the show, some owners use razor-sharp combs to tear away at the insides of the dogs' ears and the tops of their heads. They thin the dogs' natural furriness into an unnatural trimness. Then they forcefully squeeze the dogs' ears into the tulip shape considered fashionable for collies. Each breed had its own form of torment. Compared to some grooming practices, Lad's brushing and bathing were a pleasure!

Few of these ruthlessly "prepared" dogs were personal pets. Most of them were "kennel dogs," dogs bred and raised the same way prize hogs or chickens were bred and raised. The dogs were herded together in kennels, like so many prize cattle. Intelligence, loyalty, devotion—the human side of a dog—were completely ignored in the effort to breed the perfect physical animal. The body was everything; the heart and mind were nothing. Owners who wanted only to win blue ribbons at dog shows rarely bothered training, loving, or even getting to know their dogs. But before they left home on the first morning of the show, The Mistress and The Master knew none of this.

Lad, however, refused to eat a bite of his breakfast, for his throat was filled with fear of the future. And though he usually enjoyed car rides, that morning he crawled, rather than sprang, into the back seat. All the way up the drive, Lad's great, mournful eyes were turned back toward the house. He knew that the car was whizzing him along toward some dreaded fate. He was heartsick.

The big collie buried his head in The Mistress's lap and crouched hopelessly at her feet as the car chugged toward the city. All The Mistress's pettings could not awaken Lad from his despair. This was the time when he usually took his morning walk, at the heels of one of his two gods. But today, these gods were carrying him away to something very unpleasant.

In an hour or so, the ride ended, as the car drew up to Madison Square Garden. At The Master's word, Lad stepped down from the back seat onto the sidewalk. He stood there, sniffing. The roar of the city was painful to his sensitive ears, which were used to the deep silences of forest and lake. Through this din he caught the muffled noise of many dogs barking and howling.

Lad had bravely fought invaders and even risked his own life to save another. But now the collie trembled in fear. He looked up at The Mistress, with sorrowful appeal in his eyes. Her gentle touch and beloved voice finally convinced him to go into the building. If his gods were leading him to death, it was his duty to follow them without question.

Before letting Lad walk onto the floor of the show, a yawning veterinarian gave him a quick glance. Since the dog showed no outward signs of disease, the vet let him pass without even touching him. Perhaps he would have turned away some dogs—if he'd bothered to look. But he didn't.

Although vets were paid to inspect all dogs to prevent the spread of disease, during this and other shows, dogs always ended up catching diseases from one another. Later they spread the diseases to other dogs in their home kennels. As a result, dozens of dogs—including many who didn't even attend the shows—died. It's one of the risks that dog exhibitors must take. Or rather, it's one that their unlucky dogs must take.

As Lad passed in through the doorway, he halted in dismay. Dogs. Dogs. DOGS! More than two thousand of them, from Great Danes to toy terriers! And all were displayed in row after row of small cages, stretching across the vast floor space of the Garden. Lad had never known there were so many dogs on earth. At least five hundred of them were barking or howling. The terrible sound swelled to the Garden's roof and echoed back again, like countless hammers pounding Lad's eardrums.

The Mistress stood holding Lad's chain and petting the bewildered dog, while The Master went to get an attendant. Lad pressed his shaggy body closer to The Mistress's knee for comfort, as he gazed around.

There were several large wire enclosures in the Garden's center. Inside each enclosure were table, a chair, and a judging platform, which was about six inches high and four feet square. The central space was surrounded by alleys lined with platforms, which stood two feet off the ground. These platforms were divided into long rows of compartments that were only three feet in area. Each of these cells was to be the living space of some unfortunate dog for the next four days and nights. The dogs were chained into them.

The Master came back with an attendant. Lad was led through row upon row of yapping and snapping dogs of all breeds, to a section at the Garden's northeast corner. Here, in large black letters on a white sign, was inscribed COLLIES. They finally stopped in front of a compartment numbered 658. "Up, Laddie!" said The Mistress, touching the straw that covered the hard floor of the cell.

At this command, Lad usually sprang with the lightness of a cat. Now, he very slowly climbed into the horrible cell, which was to be his only resting spot for four long days. There he was chained as though he were a runaway puppy. The insult bit to the depths of his soul. He curled down in the straw. The Mistress made him as comfortable as she could. She set before him the breakfast she had brought and asked the attendant to bring him some water.

Meanwhile, The Master met a collie breeder he knew. Together they were walking along the collie section, examining the dogs. The Master had previously visited several other dog shows. But now that Lad was on exhibition, he studied the other collies with new eyes.

"Look!" he boasted to his companion, stopping in front of a platform that contained a half-dozen dogs from a single well-known kennel. "These fellows can't measure up to old Lad. See how their noses are tapered, like toothpicks. The span of their heads isn't as wide as my palm, their eyes are little and slanty, and their bodies are curved like a greyhound's. Compared with Lad, some of them are freaks. That's all they are, just freaks. Not all of them, of course, but a lot of them."

The collie breeder laughed at his friend. "Don't you know that nowadays collies are bred with narrow heads and graceful, small bones? What's the use of having brains and scenting power? These days, collies are used only for show or kept as pets—not to herd sheep. Today's fashion demands a long nose and narrow head."

"But Lad once tracked my footsteps two miles through a snowstorm," bragged The

Master. "And he understands the meaning of every simple word. He—"

"So?" said the collie breeder, unimpressed. "Very interesting, but not useful in a show. Let's have a look at your dog. Where is he?"

They met the worried Mistress as they walked down the alley toward Cell 658. "Lad won't eat a thing," she reported. "He drinks plenty of water, but he won't eat. I'm afraid he's sick."

"They hardly ever eat at a show," the collie breeder consoled her. "But they drink quarts of water. So this is your dog, eh? Hmm." He stood, legs apart, hands behind his back, gazing down at Lad. The dog was lying, head between paws, as before. He did not so much as glance up at the stranger. "Hmm," repeated the collie man thoughtfully. "Eyes too big and not slanted enough. Head too thick for length of nose. Ears too far apart. Eyes too far apart, too. Too much bone, too much bulk. Wonderful coat, though! Best coat I've seen in five years. Great tail, too! What's he entered for? Novice, eh? You may get a third place ribbon in that category."

Then the breeder added, "Yours is the true type of collie. But I'm afraid his type is too old-fashioned to compete with today's fancy show collies. Still, you never can tell. It's a pity he isn't a little more—"

"I wouldn't have him one bit different!" flashed The Mistress. "He's perfect as he is. You can't see that, though, because he isn't himself now. I've never seen him so unhappy. I wish we had never brought him here."

"You can't blame him," said the collie breeder. "Why, just suppose you were brought to a strange place like this and chained into a cage and left there four days and nights, while hundreds of other prisoners kept screaming at the top of their lungs every minute of the time! And suppose thousands of people kept jostling past your cage, night and day, pointing at you and asking you to shake hands. Would you feel very hungry or very happy?"

"If I'd known—if we'd known—" began The Mistress.

"Most of these folks know!" the collie breeder explained. "They do it year after year. There's a mighty strong lure in a bit of ribbon. Why, look what an exhibitor will do for it! He'll risk his dog's health and make his dog's life a horror. He'll ship him a thousand miles in a tight crate from show to show. Well, good luck with 658." Then the man walked on, looking at the other collies.

The Mistress, trying to blink back tears, was bending over Lad, petting him and whispering to him.

The Master watched a kennel owner hold down a nearby collie, while a second man trimmed the scared dog's feet and ankle fur. Nearly every dog but Lad had clipped ankles. At a nearby cell, a woman was sifting almost a pound of talcum powder into her dog's fur to make the coat fluffier. Other weird preparations were underway in other cages. Lad's only preparation had been baths and brushing! The Master began to feel like a fool.

As people all along the row of collie cages put finishing touches on the poor beasts, the collie breeder strolled back to 658. "The Novice Class in collies is going to be called in a little while," he told The Mistress. "Where's your exhibition leash and choke collar? I'll help you put them on."

"Why, we have only this chain, which we bought yesterday," said The Mistress. "This is his regular collar. Do we have to have a different kind?"

"You don't have to unless you want to," said the collie breeder. "But it's best to use a choke collar. It makes the dog carry its head in a fine, proud fashion that counts a lot with some judges. Makes the dog look showy, too, and keeps him from slumping. Can't slump much if you're trying not to choke, you know."

"It's horrible! Horrible!" shuddered The Mistress. "I wouldn't put such a thing on Lad for all the prizes on earth. I thought dog shows were a real treat to dogs. But now I see they're—"

"Your class is called!" interrupted the collie breeder. "Keep his head high, and keep him moving as showily as you can. Don't be scared if any of the other dogs in the ring happens to fly at him. The attendants will look out for all that. Good luck."

The Garden had begun to fill with visitors, and soon the ring was surrounded by spectators. As usual, the collie classes were among those to be judged on the first day of the show.

The unhappy Mistress guided the unhappier Lad down the aisle, through a wire gate, and into the northeastern ring. Six other Novice dogs were already there. A clerk sat at a table behind piles of multicolored ribbons. An elderly little man in tweeds stood beside the platform. He had been chosen as judge for the collie division. His name was Angus McGilead, and he was a man with stubborn opinions of his own about dogs.

At the judge's order, the Novice collies were paraded around the ring. They were beautiful creatures. Unlike Lad, most were handled by professional kennel men, not by loving owners.

They stepped high and fast, and carried their heads up. Their thin choke collars cut deep into their furry necks.

Lad moved solemnly along at The Mistress's side. He did not pant or prance or look showy. He was miserable, and every line of his magnificent body showed his misery. The Mistress, glancing at the showier dogs, wanted to cry—not because she was about to lose, but because Lad was about to lose. Again, she blamed herself bitterly for bringing him here.

McGilead stood sucking at an empty pipe and scanning the parade that circled around him. Soon he stepped up to The Mistress and said to her with a sort of sorrowful kindness, "Please take your dog over to the far end of the ring. Take him into the corner, where he won't be in my way while I am judging."

Yes, he spoke politely enough. But The Mistress would rather he had slapped her across the face. She meekly obeyed his command and went to the farthest corner of the ring. Poor Lad walked beside her. He had been disgraced, weeded out of the competition at the very start. There, far out of the contest, The Mistress stood sadly, feeling as though everyone were sneering at her dear dog's disgrace.

Lad seemed to sense her sorrow. As he stood beside her, he whined softly and licked her hand as if in encouragement. She ran her fingers along his silky head. Then, to keep from crying, she watched the other contestants.

These were no longer parading. One at a time, and then in twos, the judge stood them on the platform. He looked at their teeth. He pressed their heads between his hands. He hoisted them up by their hips. He ran his fingers through their coats. He pressed his palm upward against their underbodies. But he did all these things with such a quick and sure touch that not even the crankiest of them could complain. Then he stepped back and studied the collies. After that, McGilead seemed to remember Lad.

The judge slouched across the ring to where The Mistress was petting her dear, disgraced dog. Lazily, McGilead ran his hand over Lad, with none of the thoroughness that had marked his inspection of the other dogs. It seemed there was no need to look for the finer points in a disqualified collie. The examination lasted less than three seconds. At its end, the judge jotted down a number on a pad he held. Then he laid one hand heavily on Lad's head, and briskly thrust out his other hand at The Mistress.

"Can I take him away now?" she asked.

"Yes," rasped the judge. "And take this along with him." In his outstretched hand fluttered a little bunch of dark blue silk, with gold lettering on it. The blue ribbon! First prize in the Novice Class! And this grouchy little judge was awarding it to Lad!

The Mistress looked very hard at the ribbon in her fingers. She saw it through a strange mist. Then, as she stooped to fasten it to Lad's collar, she kissed the top of the collie's head. "It's a victory after all!" she exclaimed joyously, as she rejoined the delighted Master at the ring gate. "But, oh, it was terrible for a minute or two, wasn't it?"

Now, Angus McGilead, who had recently moved to New York from Scotland, was an expert on collies. It was this very fact that made him a bad dog-show judge, as the Kennel Club soon discovered. McGilead had little patience with the ultra-modern, inbred collies that had so completely departed from their ancestral standards. At one glance, he had recognized Lad as a dog that brought back to him the magic of the Scottish Highlands. He had noticed the deep chest, the mighty shoulders, the tiny white paws, the incredible coat, the grand head, and the soulful eyes. This was the kind of dog that a Highland master would no sooner sell than he would sell his own child. And so, McGilead had waved Lad aside while he judged the lesser dogs of his class. He did this so that he would not be tempted to look too much at Lad, and too little at them. Finally, he rejoiced to give honor where honor was due.

As the dull hours wore on that day, Lad lay, miserable, in his cell. The Guest Law did not allow him to growl at the stream of visitors who flowed past, and who sometimes paused to pat him. But he refused to look at any of them. Lad had only one thing to be happy about. It seemed he had done something that made both The Master and The Mistress very, very proud of him. Even the collie breeder seemed to regard him with more approval than before. And two or three exhibitors came over for a special look at him.

From one of these exhibitors, The Mistress learned of a dog-show rule that was new to her. The winning dog in each class must return later to the ring to compete in the Winners' class. This special competition was to determine which was the best collie among all the winners.

The Master's heart sank at this news. "I'm sorry!" he said. "You see, it's one thing to win as a novice against a bunch of untried dogs, and another to compete against the best dogs in the show. I wish we could get out of it."

"Never mind!" answered The Mistress. "Laddie has won his ribbon. They can't take that away from him. There's a silver cup for the

Winners' class, though. I wish there had been one for the Novices."

The day wore on. At last, the call came for "Winners!" And for the second time, poor Lad plodded into the ring with The Mistress. But now, instead of competing with inexperienced dogs, he was challenged by the most experienced, most prized collies in the world. Lad's heartsickness showed even more in such company. It hurt The Mistress to see him so miserable. She thought of the three days and nights to come, the nights when she and The Master could not be with him. And she had brought this upon him for the sake of a blue ribbon! The Mistress came to a sudden and very unsportsmanlike decision.

Again, the dogs paraded the ring. Again, the judge studied them from between half-shut eyes. But this time he did not wave Lad to one side. During the day, The Mistress noticed that McGilead always signaled his decisions by first laying his hand on the victor's head. Breathless, she watched for such a gesture.

The dogs were weeded out one by one until only two remained. Of these two, one was Lad, and the other was Champion Coldstream Guard. Coldstream Guard was a grand dog, perfect of coat and line, combining all that was best in the old and new styles of collies. He carried his head high with no help from the choke collar. His perfectly shaped ears hung at exactly the right curve.

Lad and Coldstream Guard were placed shoulder to shoulder on the platform. Even The Mistress could not fail to contrast her pet's sorrowful attitude with the Champion's alert beauty. "Lad!" she whispered as McGilead compared the two. "Laddie, we're going home. Home! Home, Lad!"

Home! At the word, a thrill went through the great dog. Up went his head and his ears. His dark eyes glowed with eagerness as he looked up at The Mistress. Home! Yet, despite the change in Lad's expression, the other was the finer dog from a show viewpoint. The Mistress could see he was. Even the new, upward tilt of Lad's ears could not make them as perfect in shape as Coldstream Guard's.

With almost a gesture of regret, McGilead laid his hand on Coldstream Guard's head. The Mistress read the verdict, and she accepted it. "Come, Laddie, dear," she said tenderly. "At least, you're second—a Reserve Winner. That's something."

"Wait!" snapped McGilead. The judge was holding one of Champion Coldstream Guard's shapely ears and turning it backward. His fingers, falling on the dog's head, had met an odd stiffness in the curve of the ear. Now he began to examine that ear, and then the other. In this way, he uncovered a clever bit of bandaging.

There were a number of strips of tape inside each of the dog's ears. That's why Champion Coldstream Guard's ears were shaped so perfectly! But using tape to hold down a dog's ears was cheating. McGilead looked at the dog. Then he looked long and hard at the man who was holding the leash and fidgeting nervously under the judge's glare.

Finally, McGilead laid both hands on Lad's great, honest head, almost as in blessing. "Your dog wins, madam," he said. "And while it is not a judge's duty to say so, I am glad. I won't insult you by asking if he is for sale. But if you ever have to part with—" He did not finish, but quickly gave The Mistress the Winning Class ribbon. And now, as Lad left the ring, hundreds of hands reached out to pat him. All at once he was a celebrity.

Without returning the dog to his cell, The Mistress went directly to the collie breeder. "When do they present the cups?" she asked.

"Not until Saturday night, I believe," said this man. "I congratulate you both on—"

"So in order to win his cup, Lad will have to stay in this—this hell for three more days and nights?"

"Of course. All the dogs—"

"And if he doesn't stay, he won't get the cup?"

"No. It would go to the Reserve Winner, I suppose, or to—"

"Good!" declared The Mistress in relief. "Then Lad can keep his two ribbons without cheating any other dogs."

"What do you mean?" asked the puzzled collie breeder.

But The Master understood and approved. "Good!" The Master said. "I wanted to suggest it to you all day, but I didn't have the nerve. Come around to the Exhibitors' Entrance. I'll go ahead and start the car."

"But what's the idea?" asked the collie breeder in confusion.

"The idea," replied The Mistress, "is that the silver cup can go to any dog that wants it. Lad's coming home. He knows it, too. Just look at him. I promised him he would go home. We can get there by dinner time, and he has a day's fast to make up for."

"But," protested the collie breeder, "if you withdraw your dog like that, the Association will never allow you to exhibit him at its shows again."

"The Association can keep its pretty silver cup," The Mistress replied. "Maybe it will cheer up the Association since it's losing Lad. As for showing him again—well, I wouldn't lose these two ribbons for a hundred dollars. But I wouldn't put my worst enemy's dog through the torture of winning them over again. Come along, Lad, we're going back home."

At the magic word, Lad broke his silence for the first time that day. He broke it with a series of thunderous barks that put to shame the puny noise-making efforts of every other dog in the show.

CHAPTER 6

Lost!

The Master went out first to get the car and bring it around to the Garden's side exit. The Mistress gathered up Lad's belongings and followed, along with Lad himself. She left the huge, noisy building, with Lad pacing happily at her side.

At the exit, The Mistress was forced to leave a deposit of five dollars, "to insure the return of the dog to his cell." She did this, although she had no intention of bringing Lad back to the show. Then she was told the law required that all dogs in New York City streets be muzzled.

It was no use explaining that Lad would be in the streets only as long as it took for the car to travel to the ferry. The door attendant insisted that the law must be obeyed. So The Mistress reluctantly bought a muzzle. It was a big, awkward thing, made of steel and attached with leather straps. It looked like a rattrap. And it fenced in the dog's nose and mouth with shiny metal bars.

To Lad, this muzzle was horrible. Not even the touch of The Mistress's dear fingers as she adjusted the thing to his head could lessen the humiliation. And the fact that it was painful made it worse. The huge dog tried to dislodge the muzzle with his small white forepaws. He tried to rub it off against The Mistress's skirt. But he could not budge it.

Lad looked up at The Mistress pleadingly. All his life she had given him gentleness, affection, and understanding. Yet today, she had brought him to this terrible place. And now, just as the ordeal seemed about to end, she was tormenting him with this contraption. Lad did not rebel. But he begged. And The Mistress understood.

"Laddie, dear!" she whispered, as she led him across the sidewalk to where The Master waited with the car. "Laddie, old friend, I'm just as sorry about it as you are. But it's only for a few minutes. Just as soon as we get to the ferry, we'll take it off and throw it into the river. I promise. It's only for a few minutes."

The Mistress, for once, was mistaken. Lad was to wear the hated muzzle for much, much longer than "a few minutes."

"Give Lad the back seat to himself, and come sit in front with me," suggested The Master, as The Mistress and Lad met him at the car. "The poor old chap has been so cramped up all day that he'll like a whole seat to stretch out on." So The Mistress opened the door and motioned Lad to the back seat. The collie jumped up on the cushion and sat down. The Mistress got into the front seat with The Master. And the car set out on its six-mile run to the ferry.

Now that his face was turned homeward, Lad might have become interested in his new surroundings. But the horrible muzzle absorbed all his feelings. He was a country dog, this giant collie, with his mighty shoulders and shaggy coat and mournful eyes. He had never been in a city before. The swirl of countless noises, smells, and lights were all jarringly new to him. So were the masses of people on the sidewalk, and the tangle of traffic through which The Master was threading the car's way with such difficulty. But of all the day's new experiences, the muzzle was the most sickening.

Lad was certain The Mistress did not realize how the muzzle was hurting him, or how he hated it. Since she had never been unkind to him, it must be she did not understand. She had never taught him a Muzzle Law. So Lad felt justified in trying again to remove the painful thing. He pawed it, first with one foot, and then with both. He could jiggle it from side to side, but that was all. And each shift of the steel bars hurt his tender nose more than the one before. Lad tried to rub it off against the seat cushion, with the same sad result.

Lad looked up at the backs of his gods, and whined very softly. But the city was so noisy that Lad's soft whimper went unheard. Neither The Mistress nor The Master turned around to speak to the sufferer. They were in a traffic jam that called for all their attention. It was no time for talking to or petting a dog. Lad got to his feet and stood on the slippery leather cushion. Trying to keep his balance, he rubbed the muzzle against one of the car's roof supports. Working away with all his might, he tried to get enough leverage to pry the muzzle loose.

Just then, there was a brief gap in the traffic. The Master sped up, darted ahead of a delivery truck, and turned sharply into a side street. The car's sudden twist made Lad lose his balance, and threw him against one of the rear doors. The door, which hadn't been properly shut, could not withstand the eighty-pound impact. It burst open. And Lad was thrown out onto the street.

He landed on his side in the roadway, with a force that knocked the breath out of him. Directly above his head glared the twin lights of the delivery truck The Master had just shot past. The truck was going at a good twelve miles an hour. And the dog had fallen within six feet of its fat front wheels.

Even as the tires grazed his fur, Lad gathered himself together, his feet well under him, and sprang far to one side. The truck missed him—though by only a few inches. His leap brought him scrambling out of the truck's way, but on the wrong side of the avenue, and under the fender of a car that was going in the opposite direction.

Once again, an instinctive leap saved the dog from death. Then Lad stopped and stared around in search of his gods. But not even a trained human eye could have recognized a specific car in that blur of swerving traffic.

By now, The Mistress and The Master were half a block away, down a less crowded side street. They were making up for lost time by speeding ahead. Then they turned into the next westbound street. They did not look back, for there was a car directly in front of them, and The Master was trying to pass it safely. In fact, neither The Master nor The Mistress turned around to speak to Lad until they had reached the lower end of Riverside Drive. This was nearly a mile to the north.

Meanwhile, Lad was standing, confused and panting, in the middle of Columbus Circle. Millions of cars seemed to be whizzing directly at him from every direction at once. But even as he tried to dodge traffic, his frightened eyes and his pulsing nostrils kept searching for The Mistress and The Master. Lad's eyes told him only that a number of cars were likely to kill him. But his nose told him that there were fields and woods and water nearby. So Lad wove his way toward those familiar odors.

By a miracle, he safely crossed Columbus Circle. Then he came to a standstill on a sidewalk beside a low, gray, stone wall. Behind the wall, his nose taught him, lay miles of meadows and woods and lakes. This was Central Park. But the smell of the park brought him no scent of The Mistress or of The Master. And he craved them even more than his beloved countryside. So he continued along the sidewalk for a few yards, confused, alert, watching in every direction. Seeing a figure that looked familiar, he dashed at top speed, eastward, for half a block.

Then, tricked by a passing car that looked familiar, he stepped out into the middle of the busy street. The car was traveling at twenty miles an hour. But Lad caught up with it in less than a block. As he came alongside the car, he glanced up and saw that his chase was useless. So he made his danger-filled way to the sidewalk once more. And there he stood, bewildered, heartsick, lost!

The average dog might have continued to waste energy by running hopefully up to every stranger he met, then slinking off and searching again. But Lad was too wise for that. He knew he was lost. His beloved Mistress and Master had somehow left him all alone in this crazy place. Lad stood there, hopeless, head and tail drooping, his great heart dead within him. After a while, he realized that he was still wearing the hated muzzle. In the stress of the past few minutes, Lad had actually forgotten the pain and annoyance of the thing. Now, the memory of it came back, adding to his despair.

Just as a sick animal creeps into the woods to be alone, the heartsick Lad turned to the stretch of countryside he'd scented. He jumped over the gray wall and came to earth among the shrubs along the south boundary of Central Park. Here there were also people and cars. But they were few, and far off. Surrounded by a grateful darkness and aloneness, Lad lay down on the dead grass and panted.

Through his sorrow and the nagging pain from his muzzle, Lad began to realize that he was tired. The nightmare of the dog show had worn down his nerves. The hazards of the past half-hour had made him even more exhausted. He had eaten nothing all day. He was still not hungry, for a dog must have peace of mind to be hungry. But he was terribly thirsty.

Lad got up and trotted wearily toward the Central Park lake. Soggy ice still covered the lake, but the mild weather had left half an inch of water on top of it. Lad stooped to drink. But he could not. For the steel hinge on the muzzle had become jammed and would not open. So Lad could not open his mouth wide enough to lap up any water. After trying very hard, he finally managed to stick out the end of his tongue and touch the water with it. But it was a painfully slow process, drinking water drop by drop in this way. More through tiredness than because his thirst was eased, he finally stopped and turned away from the lake.

Lad spent the next half-hour in another totally useless effort to rid himself of his muzzle. After this, the dog lay down, panting and thirsty once more. Another journey to the lake and another frustrating effort to drink, and the poor dog's brain began to work.

He no longer let himself notice the muzzle. Experience had taught him he could not dislodge it. Nor could he hope to find The Mistress and The Master. Knowing these things, his mind went on to the next step. Home! The Place—where his happy life had been spent, where his two gods lived, where there was no noise or smell or danger as here in New York. Home!

Lad stood up. He breathed deeply, and he turned around slowly, head up, nostrils quivering. He stood like this for a full minute. Then he lowered his head and trotted westward. No longer did he move uncertainly, but with as much sureness as if he were crossing the forest behind The Place, where he had roamed since puppyhood.

Lad jogged toward the northwest, and in half a mile he came to the low western wall of Central Park. Without turning aside to seek a gate, he cleared the wall and found himself on Eighth Avenue. Keeping on the sidewalk, Lad moved along to the next westward street and turned down it toward the Hudson River. He moved so calmly and certainly that no one would have taken him for a lost dog.

A patrolman on his way to the West Sixty-ninth Street police station was so taken up by his own lofty thoughts that he never even glanced at the big, mud-spattered dog that padded past him. After the patrolman reached the police station, he learned that a man and woman had just been there. They were offering a fifty-dollar reward to anyone finding a big collie named "Lad." But since the patrolman hadn't noticed Lad, he lost out on a chance to add fifty dollars to his monthly pay.

As the dog reached Amsterdam Avenue, a high little voice squealed delightedly at him. A three-year-old child was crossing the avenue, guided by her mother, a fat woman in black. As Lad was jogging by, the child suddenly flung herself upon Lad, and wrapped both arms around his shaggy neck. "Why, doggie!" she cried happily. "Why, dear, dear doggie!"

Now, Lad was in a hurry to get home, but his big heart went out to the child's hug. His tail wagged in glad friendliness; his muzzled nose tried to kiss the little face. The child tightened her hug and laid her rosy cheek close to his own. "I love you, Miss Doggie!" she whispered in Lad's ear.

Then the fat woman in black bore down upon them. Fiercely, she yanked the child away from the dog. Then, seeing that the mud on Lad's shoulder had dirtied the child's white coat, the woman swung her bag and brought it down hard on the dog's head.

Lad winced under the heavy blow. Then hot anger blazed through him. But since this unpleasant, fat creature was not a man, The Law allowed him only to bare his teeth and growl a warning from far down in his throat. Frightened, the woman shrank back and screamed loudly. In an instant, a patrolman was beside her.

"What's wrong, ma'am?" asked the patrolman.

The woman pointed a fat forefinger at Lad, who had taken up his journey again and was halfway across the street. "Mad dog!" she sputtered. "He—he bit me! Bit at me, anyhow!"

Without waiting to hear the last sentence, the patrolman chased after Lad. Here was a chance to be a hero. As he ran, he pulled out his pistol.

Lad had reached the western side of Amsterdam Avenue and turned onto a side street beyond it. He was not hurrying, but his trot quickly ate up distances. So by the time the patrolman reached the west corner, the dog was nearly half a block ahead. The officer, still running, leveled his pistol and fired. The bullet flew high and to the right, smashing a second-story window and echoing through the narrow street.

"What's up?" excitedly asked a boy, hanging on the corner with a group of buddies.

"Mad dog!" puffed the policeman as he sped past. The boys joined happily in the chase, outdistancing the officer, just as he fired a second shot.

Lad felt a white-hot ridge of pain cut along his left flank. He wheeled to face his enemy, and he found himself looking at a half-dozen boys, who charged down on him. Behind the boys plodded a man in blue, who was carrying something bright. Lad disliked this sort of attention. He wheeled around again and continued running west, now at a faster pace. The boys broke into louder yells, and three or four new recruits joined them. The yap of "Mad dog! Mad dog!" filled the air.

Lad crossed Broadway and galloped down the hill toward Riverside Park. The shouting crowd followed at his heels. Twice the patrolman got in front of the hunt, and twice he fired, both bullets going wide.

Fleeing at top speed, Lad turned down a street and onto a pier that jutted a hundred feet out into the Hudson River. The collie flew along this pier, determined that these howling New Yorkers not prevent him from going home. The clattering boys and policeman followed Lad onto the pier. As Lad flashed by, a dock watchman threw a heavy beam of wood at the dog. It whizzed past, narrowly missing Lad's hind legs.

Lad reached the end of the pier. Behind him raced the crowd—sure it had at last cornered the dangerous brute. The collie stopped for a moment, glancing to the north and to the south. Everywhere the wide river stretched away. It must be crossed for him to get home. And there was only one way for him to cross it.

The watchman, hard at Lad's heels, raised the club he carried. Down came the club with murderous force—landing upon the spot where Lad had been standing. But Lad was no longer there. One great bound had carried him over the edge and into the black water below.

Down he plunged into the river and far, far under it. Then he started fighting his way back to the surface. The water that gushed into his mouth and nostrils was salty and polluted, not at all like the water from the lake at the edge of The Place. It made him sick. And the February chill of the river cut into him like a million needles.

Lad came to the surface, and struck out bravely for the opposite shore, which was more than a mile away. As his head appeared, a yell went up from the gang standing at the end of the pier. Bits of wood and coal began to shower the water all around him. A pistol shot plopped into the river only six inches away. But for the humans, the light was bad, and the river was a tossing mass of blackness. So the dog was able to swim, unhurt, beyond the range of the objects thrown at him.

Normally, a swim of one or two miles was not difficult for Lad, even in ice-cold water. But this water was not like any he had ever known. The tide was turning, and the currents battered him about. And there were pieces junk that kept looming up just in front of him and banging against his sides. Once a small ship passed less than thirty feet ahead of him. Its wake caught the dog, sucked him under, and spun him around before he could fight clear of it.

Lad's lungs were bursting. He was worn out. The bullet wound was hurting him, and the salt water bit into it. The muzzle half-blinded and half-smothered him. But because of his heroic heart, Lad kept on. He swam for an hour or more, until his body and brain were numb. Only the mechanical action of his muscles kept him in motion.

After what seemed like a lifetime of effort, his forepaws felt solid ground. With his last ounce of strength, Lad crawled ashore at the base of the Palisades. There, he collapsed and lay shivering, struggling for breath.

Lad lay there a long time, letting Nature bring back some of his wind and his strength. His shaggy body ached terribly. Then, once he was able to move again, Lad continued on his journey. Sometimes swimming, sometimes running on the ground, he skirted the Palisades until he found one of the paths that led up to the top of the cliff. He made his way up this path slowly, conserving his strength as best he could. At the top, Lad lay down again to rest. Behind him and across the river rose the inky skyline of the city. Ahead was flat ground with a downward slope beyond it.

Getting to his feet once more, Lad stood still and sniffed the air. Having found the direction of home, he traveled westward down the slope and then across the endless salt marshes. Sometimes he traveled on roads or paths, sometimes across fields or hills. But he always traveled in a straight line.

It was a little before midnight when he came to the hills above Hackensack, New Jersey. He continued to lumber, head low, through a darkened village. Now it was the muzzle that bothered him most. It felt as if it were made of hornet stingers and burning iron that weighed a ton. As often happens with sensitive dogs, the muzzle was beginning to do strange things to his brain. Thirst, unbearable thirst, was also torturing Lad. But he could not drink at the pools and brooks he crossed. For the muzzle's steel hinge had become jammed, so he couldn't open his mouth wide enough even to pant.

Just then, from out of the shadows, a monstrous shape hurled itself on Lad. A mongrel watchdog had been dozing on his owner's doorstep when the pad-pad-pad of Lad's feet sounded on the road. During the journey, other dogs had run out to yap or growl at the wanderer. But because Lad was big and followed an unswerving course, they never attacked him. This mongrel was less cautious. Or perhaps he realized that the muzzle made Lad powerless. At any rate, he gave no warning bark or growl.

Lad's first notice of the attack was a flying seventy-five-pound object that crashed against his flank. In the same instant, two sets of fangs sank into his shoulder. Under the onslaught, Lad fell onto his left side, his enemy upon him. Then, once Lad was down, the mongrel skillfully shifted his shoulder grip to a far more murderous hold on his fallen victim's throat.

A dog's only weapons are his teeth. So when a dog's mouth is enclosed in a muzzle, it is completely helpless. And so Lad was pitifully unable to fight back. Exhausted, flung to the earth, his mighty jaws muzzled, Lad seemed as good as dead. But a collie is not beaten just because he is down. His wolf nature guards against that. Even as he fell, Lad gathered his legs under him as he had done when he fell from the car.

Once again, he was on his feet, snarling and lunging to break the mongrel's grip on his throat. His exhaustion was forgotten as his reserve strength leaped into play. Without use of his teeth, Lad's extraordinary strength was his only defense.

Finally Lad tore loose from the mongrel's hold. The mongrel sprang at him to get a better grip. Lad reared to meet him, snapping powerlessly with his tightly locked mouth. The force of Lad's leap sent his enemy spinning backward. But the mongrel immediately attacked once again. This time he did not give his enemy a chance to rear, but instead sprang at Lad's flank. Lad wheeled to meet the rush. Using his shoulder, he was able to break its force.

Because he was helpless to fight his enemy, it might have made sense for Lad to try to outrun him. If he stood his ground, he would eventually be torn to death. Since Lad was no fool, he knew that. Yet he ignored the chance to run away and continued to fight this hopeless battle.

Three times, Lad's intelligence and incredible quickness enabled him to block the big mongrel's rushes. But the fourth time, as Lad tried to rear up, his hind foot slipped on a slick puddle of ice. Lad went down in a heap.

And again the mongrel struck. Before the collie could regain his feet, the mongrel found a hold on the side of Lad's throat. Pinning down the muzzled dog, the mongrel continued to improve his hold by grinding his way toward the jugular vein.

But suddenly his teeth met something more solid than fur. It was a thin leather strap. The mongrel gnawed fiercely at this solid obstacle, possibly mistaking it for flesh. Lad twisted to free himself, but seventy-five pounds of fighting weight was holding his neck to the ground. All of a sudden, the mongrel growled in savage triumph. The strap was bitten through!

The victor gave one final tug on the broken leather end. For a moment, the pull drove the steel bars painfully deep into Lad's bruised nose. Then, as if by magic, the muzzle was lifted from his head. Suddenly it was dangling from the mongrel's jaws. With a motion so swift that the eye could not follow it, Lad was on his feet and plunging wildly into the battle. Through a miracle, his jaws were free; his suffering was over. The joy of freedom sent energy sweeping through him.

The mongrel dropped the muzzle and eagerly returned to battle. To his dismay, now he found himself fighting not a helpless dog, but a crazed wolf. With dizzying quickness,

Lad's head and body moved and kept on moving. And every motion meant a deep slash in his enemy's shorthaired hide.

The collie easily dodged the mongrel's awkward counterattacks, and kept on boring in. His short front teeth sank down to the enemy's bone. His fangs slashed deep, as only the wolf and collie can slash. Swept off his feet, the mongrel rolled, howling, into the road. As he did, Lad tore grimly at the enemy's exposed underbelly.

Up went a window in the shack. A man shouted. A woman in a house across the way screamed. Lad glanced up at these sounds. The wounded mongrel used this momentary break in battle to scamper back to the doorstep, yelping in terror and pain. Lad did not pursue him. Instead, he jogged along on his journey without one backward look.

After about a mile, he stopped to drink at a stream. Lad drank for ten minutes. Then he went on. With his thirst satisfied, he forgot his pain, his exhaustion, his muddy and blood-caked and torn coat, and the memory of his nightmare day. He was going Home!

At gray dawn, The Mistress and The Master turned in at the entrance to The Place. They had searched all night for Lad. They had driven from one end of Manhattan to the other, from the police headquarters to the dog pound. And now The Master was bringing his tired and heartsick wife home to rest. He, though, would return to the city to keep searching for Lad.

The car chugged down the driveway to the house. But before it had covered half the distance, the early morning stillness was shattered by a challenging bark. From his guard post on the veranda, Lad ran stiffly forward to block the way. But as he ran, his eyes and nose suddenly told him these mysterious newcomers were his gods.

With a gasp of overjoyed disbelief, The Mistress jumped down from the car before it came to a stop. She was on her knees when she caught Lad's muddy and bloody head, which she held tightly in her arms. "Oh, Lad!" she sobbed. "Laddie! Laddie!"

At this, Lad's stiffness and wounds and weariness disappeared. He tried to lick the dear face bending so tearfully above him. Then, with puppy-like joy, he rolled on the ground, waving all four dirty little feet in the air and playfully pretending to snap at the loving hands that petted him. This was ridiculous behavior for a dignified, full-grown collie. But Lad didn't care, because it made The Mistress stop crying and start to laugh. And that was what Lad most wanted her to do.

CHAPTER 7

Instinct

The Place was nine miles north of Paterson, New Jersey. Every year the great North Jersey Livestock Fair was held nearby. This fair awarded prizes for the best purebred cattle, sheep, and pigs in the area.

A wealthy Wall Street businessman liked to pretend he was a gentleman farmer. As a hobby, he spent a lot of money raising prize sheep. It was a hobby he enjoyed, but which annoyed the few friends he had. The Mistress and The Master happened to be among his unlucky friends. So when the businessman brought his sheep to the fair, he decided to break up the trip by spending a day at The Place.

Two days before the fair, a flock of twenty sheep descended from the hills, led by a grumpy-looking Scotsman named McGillicuddy. Working for the Wall Street "farmer" made the shepherd even grumpier. In northern New Jersey, live sheep are almost as rare as dinosaurs.

So a dog that does not know sheep is likely to think of them as his rightful prey. In other words, the sight of sheep has turned many an otherwise law-abiding dog into a killer. To avoid trouble, The Master decided to ship off all his collies, except Lad, to the boarding kennels, ten miles away.

"Does the old dog go, too, sir?" asked The Place's foreman, with a nod at Lad.

Lad was watching from the top of the veranda steps. The Master looked at Lad and then answered, "No. Lad has more right to be here than any useless, imported sheep. He won't bother them if I tell him not to. Let him stay."

An hour later, the grumpy McGillicuddy herded the dusty and bleating sheep down the driveway and into one of The Master's fenced-in corrals. As they turned in at the gate of The Place, Lad rose from his rug on the veranda. Outraged by the strange sight, he intended to drive the intruders out onto the main road. Head lowered, Lad ran along silently. To him, this seemed to be an emergency. For all he knew, these twenty smelly, woolly things might be fighters who would attack him. They might even threaten his gods. So, like a thunderbolt, Lad charged at the enemy.

McGillicuddy sprang quickly to the front of his flock, staff raised. But before he could make a move to hit Lad, a sweet voice called out to the dog. For as she came out onto the veranda, The Mistress saw Lad dash to the attack. "Lad!" she cried. "Lad!"

The great dog halted.

"Down!" called The Mistress. "Leave them alone! Do you hear, Lad? Leave them alone! Come back here!"

Lad heard. And Lad obeyed. Lad always obeyed.

Trembling with anger, yet with no thought of rebelling, Lad turned and trotted back to the veranda. He thrust his cold nose into The Mistress's warm little hand and looked up eagerly into her face. He hoped she would change her mind about the command to keep away from the sheep and their driver. But The Mistress only patted his head and whispered, "We don't like it any more than you do, Laddie. But we mustn't let anyone know we don't. Leave them alone!"

The twenty priceless sheep filed past the veranda and on to the corral. "I suppose they'll carry off all the prizes at the fair, won't they?" asked The Mistress politely, as McGillicuddy plodded past her.

"Maybe, aye," grunted McGillicuddy. "Maybe, nay."

As the Scot moved on, Lad strolled down toward the corral to supervise the task of locking up the sheep. The Mistress did not stop him. She felt certain her order of "Leave them alone!" had made the twenty visitors safe from him.

Lad walked slowly around the corral, his gaze on the sheep. These were the first sheep he had ever seen. Heredity is powerful in dogs, and it takes strange forms. A collie has a strain of wolf in him, and wolves killed sheep as far back as ancient times. Yet Lad's collie ancestors had herded and guarded flocks on the Scottish moors for thousands of years. Around and around the corral Lad prowled. His eyes were lit with half-memories; his sensitive nostrils quivered at the scents that enveloped them.

From time to time, McGillicuddy eyed the dog with a scowl. These sheep were his livelihood, his comfortably overpaid job with the Wall Street farmer. He was responsible for their welfare. And he did not at all like the way this collie eyed the prize sheep. McGillicuddy was also dissatisfied with the strength of the corral. Its wire fencing was rusty and sagging; its gate hung crookedly and had a crazy latch. If the flock's leader decided to press against the gate or against some of the rustier wire strands, there would soon be a gap through which the entire flock could move. And once outside—

McGillicuddy again glared at Lad.

Half an hour later, the Wall Street farmer arrived at The Place. He came in a fancy convertible. On the seat beside him sat his pasty-faced, four-year-old son. At his feet was something that appeared to be either a four-legged animal or a ragbag. Putting on their best faces, The Mistress and The Master came out to welcome the guests. Lad, who had returned from the makeshift sheep yard, stood beside them.

There was a child in the car. And though there had been few children in Lad's life, he loved them as a big-hearted dog always loves the helpless. That is why, at sight of this child, Lad rejoiced. But the animal crouching at the Wall Street farmer's feet was a different form of guest. Lad recognized the thing as a dog, but unlike any dog he had ever seen. An unpleasant-looking dog. Just as the little boy was an unpleasant-looking child.

"Well!" announced the Wall Street farmer as he scrambled out of the car. "Here I am! The sheep got here all safe? Good! I knew they would. McGillicuddy's a genius—nothing he can't do with sheep. You remember my son, Mortimer? He begged so much to come along, his mother said I'd better bring him. I knew you'd be glad. Shake hands with the nice people, Morty, darling."

"I won't!" snarled the not-so-darling Morty, hanging back.

Then the boy caught sight of Lad. The collie came straight up to the child, grinning from ear to ear. As he did, the collie wrinkled his nose so delightedly that all his white front teeth showed. Morty flung himself forward to greet the huge dog. But the Wall Street farmer, with a shout of warning, caught the boy in his arms and bravely thrust his own fat body between Mortimer and Lad.

"What does the beast mean by snarling at my son?" demanded the Wall Street farmer. "You people have no right to let such a vicious dog roam free."

"He's not snarling," The Mistress declared. "He's smiling. That's Lad's way. Why, he'd let himself be cut up into squares sooner than hurt a child."

Still doubtful, the Wall Street farmer cautiously set down his son on the veranda. Morty threw himself on Lad, hauling and mauling the collie this way and that. If any adult had treated Lad this way, he would have soon buried his fangs in him. Indeed, The Master now gazed nervously at Lad and the boy. But The Mistress was not worried about her pet's behavior. And The Mistress, as always, was right.

Lad happily endured the mauling. He even tried to kiss the boy's pale little face. Morty repaid this attention by slapping Lad across the mouth. Lad only wagged his tail and snuggled closer to the child. Meanwhile, the Wall Street farmer was loudly calling attention to the second of the two treasures he had brought along. "Melisande!" he cried.

At the summons, the fuzzy monstrosity that had been left in the car stopped scowling at Lad and cast a glance at its owner. It looked like a cross between an Old English sheepdog and a dachshund. Straw-colored fur covered the scrawny body. A thin tail hung limply between crooked hind legs. Evil little eyes peered out from beneath a stubble of head fringe. It had a pretty name. But it was not a pretty dog.

"What in blazes is he?" asked The Master.

"She is a Prussian sheepdog," the Wall Street farmer proudly replied. "She is the first of her breed ever imported to America. Cost me $1,100 to buy her from a Chicago man, who brought her over from Europe. I'm going to show her at the Garden next winter. What do you think of her, old man?"

The Master started to answer, "She looks like the dishrag I bought from a traveling salesman for a dollar." But since he was the

Wall Street farmer's host, The Master instead babbled some flattering lies and watched the visitor lift the scraggly creature out of the car.

The moment she was on the ground, Melisande made a wild dash at Lad. Snarling, she snapped at his throat. Lad simply turned his shaggy shoulder to meet her attack. So Melisande found herself gripping nothing but a mouthful of his fur. Lad did not appear angered by the attack. And the Wall Street farmer dragged away Melisande by the scruff of the neck.

The $1,100 Prussian sheepdog next caught a glimpse of one of The Mistress's pet peacock chicks strutting across The Lawn. With a yap of glee, Melisande rushed off after it. The chick wasn't afraid. For the dogs of The Place had always been trained to leave the fowls alone. So the pretty little peacock fell easy prey to the first snap of Melisande's jaws.

Lad growled at this lawlessness. The Mistress bit her lip to keep her self-control at the killing of her pet peacock. The Master blurted out something. But it was drowned out by the Wall Street farmer, who was bellowing at his $1,100 treasure, trying to call it back before it killed anything else.

"Well, I'm sorry this happened," the guest said as he returned to the veranda, dragging

Melisande along behind him. "But you must overlook it. You see, Melisande is so high-spirited she is hard to control. That's the way it is with thoroughbred dogs. Don't you agree?"

The Master glanced at his wife. She was now out of earshot, having gone to pick up the dead peacock. So The Master allowed himself to speak frankly, without worrying that his wife would feel he was being an ungracious host.

"A thoroughbred dog," he said, "is either the best dog on earth, or else the worst. If he is the best, he learns to obey. He learns it without being beaten or sworn at. If he is the worst, then it's wisest for his owner to hunt up some sucker and sell the cur to him for $1,100. You'll notice I said his 'owner,' not his 'master.' There's all the difference in the world between those two terms. Anybody with money can be an owner. But all the cash in the world won't make a man a dog's master unless he's that sort of man. Think it over."

The Wall Street farmer glared at his host. Then he put a leash on Melisande and gruffly asked that she be fastened to one of the empty kennels.

The Mistress came back to the group as the gardener led the $1,100 beast to the kennel. Having recovered her self-control, The Mistress said to her guest, "I never heard of a Prussian sheepdog before. Is she trained to herd your sheep?"

"No," replied the Wall Street farmer, his anger now forgotten. "Not yet. In fact, she hates the sheep. She's young, so we haven't tried to train her for shepherding. We have taken her into the pasture a few times, but she flies at the sheep. So we keep her away from them. But by next season—"

He got no further. The sound of wailing drowned out his speech. "Morty!" exclaimed the visitor in panic. "It's Morty! Quick!" Following the sound, he ran up the veranda steps and into the house, closely followed by The Mistress and The Master.

The curious Mortimer had been busy exploring. Bored by the stupid talk of grownups and tired of Lad's friendly play, the child had slipped through the door into the living room. There, a cheerful wood fire blazed on the hearth. In front of the fireplace was an enormous soft couch. Something that looked like a dust ball was curled in the exact center of the couch.

As Mortimer came into the room with Lad at his heels, the fluffy ball lazily uncurled and stretched. In this way, it revealed itself as a furry gray kitten. This was The Mistress's moody new Persian kitten, Tipperary. With a squeal of discovery, Mortimer grabbed Tipperary and tried to pull her fluffy tail. A lightning stroke of one of her forepaws, and Tipperary was free. Satisfied, the kitten moved to the far end of the couch and lay down there to renew her nap.

Morty stood blinking in amazement as four red marks appeared on the back of his hand. Then a mad fury fired his brain. Screaming in rage, he took hold of the cat by the nape of the neck and stamped toward the fireplace with her. He drew back his arm to fling the kitten into the flames.

That's when Lad stepped in.

Now, Lad was not at all interested in Tipperary. He probably didn't even realize what Morty planned to do. But one thing he did realize: a silly child was toddling straight toward the fire. As many another wise dog has done, Lad quietly stepped between Morty and the hearth. But Mortimer had walked toward the hearth so quickly that the dog had to stand quite close to the fire to block him. Thus, Lad found the heat from the burning logs almost unbearable. It bit through his thick coat and into the tender flesh beneath. But like a rock, he kept standing there.

Mortimer screamed even louder, frustrated that Lad was thwarting his plan to kill the kitten. Now he tried throwing the kitten over Lad's tall back and into the fire. But Tipperary fell short. As she landed on the dog's shoulders, she dug in her claws. Then she leapt to the floor. From there, she sprang to the top of the bookshelves, spitting back angrily at Mortimer.

Morty's interest in the fire had been purely as a way to kill the cat. But finding his path to it blocked, he decided to go there himself. As the child tried to toddle around Lad, the dog took a forward step that again barred the way. Morty went wild with frustration. His howls reached the ears of the grownups on The Lawn. Then the child flew at Lad, beating the dog with his fists, tearing at the thick fur, stamping upon the tiny white forepaws, kicking the ribs and stomach.

The Child kept howling as he punished the dog that was saving him from death. But Lad did not move. The kicking and beating and hair pulling were not pleasant, but they were bearable. The heat was not. The smell of singed fur began to fill the room. But Lad stood firm.

Finally, the humans rushed in, the Wall Street farmer in front. Assuming that Lad had bitten his son's bleeding hand, the businessman grabbed a chair and prepared to swing it at Lad. Lad saw it coming. With lightning swiftness, he whirled to one side as the wood descended. The chair missed him by a fraction of an inch and splintered into pieces. It was an antique, and had belonged to The Mistress's great grandparents.

For the first time in his life, Lad broke the sacred Guest Law by growling at a visitor. But surely this fat bellower was no guest! Lad looked at his gods for information.

"Down, Lad!" said The Master very gently, his voice not quite steady. Confused, but obedient, Lad dropped to the floor.

"The brute tried to kill my boy!" stormed the Wall Street farmer as he caught the howling Morty up in his arms to study the wound.

He's my guest! He's my guest! HE'S MY GUEST! The Master was saying over and over to himself. *Lord, help me to remember he's my GUEST!*

The Mistress came forward. "Lad would sooner die than hurt a child," she declared, trying not to think about the wrecked chair. "He loves children. Here, let me see Morty's hand. Why, those are cat scratches!"

"The nasty cat scwatched me!" bawled Morty. "Kill her, Daddy! I twied to. I twied to frow her in the fire. But the howwible dog wouldn't let me! Kill her, Daddy! Kill the dog, too!"

The Master's mouth flew wide open.

"Won't you go down to the corral, dear," The Mistress said quickly to her husband, "and see if the sheep are all right? Take Lad along with you."

Lad was the only one of all The Place's dogs that had the run of the house. But during the rest of that day, he kept out of the way— confused, sorrowful, his burns still paining him despite The Master's care. After boasting all evening of his sheep's unmatched quality and of their certain victory in the fair, the Wall Street farmer finally agreed to go to bed. At last, silence settled over The Place.

But in the black hour before dawn, that same silence was split by a terrible outcry. It was the mingling of yells and bleats and barks and the scurry of many feet. It burst out all at once, lasted about half a minute, and then died to stillness.

By that time, everyone on The Place was out of bed. Still in pajamas, they trooped down into the lower hall. There, the Wall Street farmer was yelling and yanking at a door bolt he was unable to open. "It's my sheep!" he shouted. "That accursed dog of yours has gotten at them. He's slaughtering them. I heard the poor things bleating, and I heard him snarling among them. They cost—"

"If you're speaking of Lad," blazed The Master, furious, "he—"

"Here are the flashlights," interrupted The

Mistress. "Let me open that door for you. I understand the bolt."

Out into the dark they went, almost colliding with McGillicuddy. The Scot, awakened like the rest, had already gone to the corral. He was now coming back to report that the corral was empty and all the sheep were gone. "It's the collie!" sputtered McGillicuddy. "I swear it's him. I suspected him all along, from the way he glared at our sheep yesterday. He—"

"I said so!" roared the Wall Street farmer. "The murderous brute! First he tries to kill Morty. And now he slaughters my sheep. You—"

The Master started to speak. But in the darkness, a little hand was laid gently across his mouth.

"You told me he always slept under the piano!" accused the guest, as the four made their way toward the corral. "Well, I looked there just now. He isn't under the piano. He—he—"

"Lad!" called The Master. And then, at the top of his lungs, "Lad!"

A distant growl, a snarl, a yelp, and soon Lad appeared in the farthest gleam of the flashlight. He stood there for only a moment. Then he turned around and vanished in the dark. The Master didn't call him back. For the sight of Lad, standing in the glare of the flashlight, left everyone speechless. The great collie's well-groomed coat was rumpled. His eyes were fireballs. And his jaws were red with blood.

A groan from The Master, a groan of heartbreak, was the first sound from the four. The dog he loved was a killer.

"It isn't true! It isn't true!" insisted The Mistress.

The Wall Street farmer and McGillicuddy had already broken into a run. The shepherd found sheep tracks on the dewy ground and was following the trail. The guest, swearing and panting, was behind him. The Mistress and The Master followed. At every step, they peered fearfully around them for what they dreaded to see—the mangled body of a slain sheep. But they saw none. So they continued following the trail.

In a quarter mile they came to its end. All four flashlights played upon a tiny hill that rose from the meadow at the forest edge. The hill was usually green. Now it was white. A flock of sheep was huddled around its slopes, hemmed in as if by a fence. At the top of the hill sat Lad. He was sitting there, one of his forepaws pinning something to the ground.

The Wall Street farmer broke the tense silence with a babbling exclamation. "Whisht!" interrupted the shepherd, who had been circling the hill, counting the sheep. "There's no sheep gone, nor so far as I can see a single sheep hurt. The full twenty is there."

The Master's flashlight shone through a gap to the top of the hill. Pinned under Lad's gently restraining forepaw crouched the badly frightened Melisande.

After examining every sheep, McGillicuddy confirmed what The Master had suspected. Tired of being captive, Melisande had gnawed through her leash. Seeking fun, she had gone to the corral. There, she had easily loosened the gate latch. Just as she was wriggling through, Lad had appeared from the veranda. Until ten hours earlier, Lad had never seen a sheep in his life. But millions of his ancestors had made their living by skillfully herding flocks, and protecting them from predators. So now he tried to drive back the would-be killer from her prey.

Lad was a veteran of several battles and knew that Melisande was no match for him. Besides, she was a female. So when Melisande snapped at him and cut his jaw, he drove her away instead of fighting back. Meanwhile, the panicky sheep had bolted out of the corral and scattered. So

Lad started to round up the scattered sheep. He was in the midst of doing this when The Master called him. After galloping back for a moment, Lad then returned to his task.

In less than five minutes, the twenty runaways were "ringed" on the hill. While still keeping the Prussian sheepdog out of mischief, Lad established himself in the ring's center. But at that point, his instincts failed him. Having rounded up his flock, Lad had no idea what to do with them. So he simply held them there until the humans arrived.

Now McGillicuddy looked guiltily around him, as though gathering courage for an unpleasant task. Drawing a deep breath, he walked up to Lad. Dropping on one knee, McGillicuddy said, "Laddie, ye're a brave, brave dog. And a wise dog! A strong dog, Laddie! I have never met yer match this side o' Scotland. Can ye take an old fool's apology for wrongin' ye? An old fool's hand in good fellowship? 'Twill pleasure me, Laddie. Will ye let bygones be bygones, an' shake?"

Yes, the speech was ridiculous. But no one felt like laughing, not even the Wall Street farmer. The shepherd was deeply sincere. And he knew that Lad would understand him, even with his Scottish accent. And Lad did understand. Solemnly he sat up. Solemnly he laid one white forepaw in the kneeling shepherd's outstretched palm. Lad's eyes glinted in wise friendliness as they met the admiring gaze of the old man. Two born shepherds were face to face. Deep was calling unto deep.

After a while, McGillicuddy broke the spell by rising to his feet. Gruffly he turned to The Master. "There's na sense, sir," he growled, "in asking will ye sell him. But I compliment ye on him, nonetheless."

"That's right. McGillicuddy's right!" boomed the Wall Street farmer, catching only part of his shepherd's words. "Good idea! He is a fine dog. I see that now. I was prejudiced. I freely admit it. A remarkable dog. What'll you take for him? Or better yet, how would you like to swap Lad for Melisande?"

The Master's mouth again flew open. But before he could reply, The Mistress hurriedly interrupted, "Dear, we left all the doors wide open. Would you mind hurrying back ahead of us and seeing that everything is safe? And will you take Lad with you?"

CHAPTER 8

The Gold Hat

Not long afterward, this same wealthy businessman decided to amuse himself by buying an old farm ten miles north of The Place. He used his money to turn woods into picnic groves, meadows into sunken gardens, and a roomy farmhouse into a cross between a castle and a country inn. Although his name was Hamilcar Q. Glure, he liked to call himself "The Wall Street Farmer." But he really thought of himself as a god.

Having settled in the region, the Wall Street farmer played at being a country gentleman. He invited people to visit him in his new house. He built shelves in his gunroom to show off all the trophies he expected to win at country fairs. And he lorded his position of wealth over the local people. But few of the neighboring families came to visit. The local farmers did not appreciate the Wall Street farmer's superior attitude. They either grinned or swore at the way Glure treated them. And they overcharged him when he asked them to perform small services.

What really disappointed Glure, though, wasn't the emptiness of his house. It was the emptiness of his trophy shelves. His expensive imported sheep earned only a third-prize ribbon at the Paterson Livestock Show. First and second prizes went to flocks owned by lowly local folk. These were small farmers who had no money with which to import prize livestock. So they bred and developed their own sheep, using their own sound judgment. At the Hohokus Fair, the Wall Street farmer's imported bull, Tenebris, won only a second-prize ribbon. The silver cup went to a bull owned by an elderly farmer who had been breeding bulls for forty years. It was discouraging. And it was mystifying. There seemed to be a conspiracy among the rural judges to boost second-rate stock, and to turn a blind eye to the virtues of overpriced imports.

It was the same in the poultry shows and hog exhibits. It was the same at the County Fair horse-trots. At one of these trots, the Wall Street farmer personally drove his $9,000 English colt. But a long-legged gelding from New Jersey won all three races.

In time, the gunroom's shelves were bright with ribbons. But none of them was for first place. And there were no cups at all in the trophy case. It was then that the Wall Street farmer had his Great Idea.

The Hampton Dog Show was to be held on Labor Day, to raise money for the Hampton branch of the American Red Cross. Mr. Hamilcar Q. Glure had kindly donated the use of his beautiful grounds for this huge outdoor dog show. He had also donated three hundred dollars toward the costs of running the show and the prizes. Not only were the usual dog classes to be judged, but also fifteen specialty trophies were to be awarded. Having offered his grounds and the first three hundred dollars, Mr. Glure turned over the details of the show to a committee. It was the committee's duty to suggest popular specialties and to raise money for the cups.

Thus, one morning, an official letter was received at The Place. It asked The Master to enter all his dogs for the show and to contribute fifteen dollars for the purchase of a Specialty Cup.

At first, The Master did not want to take any of his collies to Hampton. The dogs had not yet grown their thick winter coats. The weather was warm. And there was always the chance that sick dogs might spread disease at a dog show. Moreover, the living room trophy shelf at The Place was already filled with cups won at similar contests. And by now, The Master had begun to dislike the Wall Street farmer.

"I believe I'll send an extra ten dollars instead of entering the show," he told The Mistress. "That will save the dogs a day of torment. What do you think?"

By way of answer, The Mistress sat down on the floor where Lad was sprawled, asleep. She ran her fingers through his ruff. The great dog's tail pounded drowsily against the floor at her touch, and he raised his head for further petting.

"Laddie's winter coat is coming in beautifully," she said at last. "I don't suppose there'll be another dog there with as magnificent a coat. Besides, the show will be outdoors. So he won't risk catching any sickness. It's only one day, so he can come home at night. And I'll be right there with him all the time. I'll even take him into the ring myself. And he won't be unhappy or lonely or—or anything."

The Mistress paused, then added, "You know how much I love having people see how handsome he is. But of course—we'll do whatever you say about it." Which, naturally, settled the matter, once and for all.

A week later, a printed copy of the specialty lists arrived. The Mistress and The Master eagerly scanned its pages. There were cups offered for the best tricolor collie, for the best mother and litter, for the collie with the finest coat, for the best collie exhibited by a woman, and for the collie whose pups had won the most prizes in other shows. At the bottom of the section, in large type, were the words: "Presented by the Honorable Hugh Lester Maury of New York City: 18-KARAT GOLD SPECIALTY CUP, FOR COLLIES (conditions to be announced later)."

"A gold cup!" sighed The Mistress. "I never heard of such a thing at a dog show. Won't it look perfectly gorgeous in the center of our trophy shelf, there with all the other cups? And—"

"Hold on!" laughed The Master. "Hold on! We haven't got it, yet. I'll enter Lad for it, of course. But so will every other collie owner who reads that announcement. Besides, even if Lad won it, I'm sure we'd need a microscope to see the thing. It will probably be the size of a thimble. Gold cups cost gold money, you know."

Then The Master added, "I don't suppose this 'Honorable Hugh Lester Maury of New York City' is squandering more than ten or fifteen dollars at most on a country dog show— even for the Red Cross. I suppose he's some Wall Street buddy that Glure has coaxed into giving a prize. I've never heard of him before. Have you?"

"No," admitted The Mistress. "But I feel I'm beginning to love him. Oh, Laddie," she confided to the dog, "I'm going to give you a bath every day till then, and brush you two hours every morning, and feed you on liver and—"

"'Conditions to be announced later,'" quoted The Master, studying the offer once more. "I wonder what that means. Of course, in a specialty show, anything goes. But—"

"I don't care what the conditions are," interrupted The Mistress. "Lad can come up to them. Why, there isn't a greater dog in America than Lad. And you know it."

"I know it," The Master agreed. "But will the judge? You might have to tell him so."

"Lad will tell him," promised The Mistress. "Don't worry."

On Labor Day morning, a thousand cars descended upon the village of Hampton. Then they chugged up a hill into the estate of Hamilcar Q. Glure, Wall Street Farmer. There, the country stillness was shattered by barks in every key. An open field had been set aside for ten double rows of platforms, to keep the show's three hundred exhibits. A banner was strung between two trees above the central show ring. It bore a blazing red cross at either end. In its center were the words WELCOME TO GLURE TOWERS!

Lad enjoyed the ten-mile spin through the morning air in the back seat of The Place's only car. However, the past week's baths and combings had made him unhappily aware that a dog show was about to take place. Now, even before the car entered the gateway of Glure Towers, the collie's ears and nose told him the time of suffering was at hand. His pleasure in the ride vanished. He looked sadly at The Mistress and tried to bury his head under her circling arm. Lad hated dog shows, as does every intelligent dog.

Parking the car, The Mistress and The Master led the unhappy dog to the clerk's desk. There they received his number tag and card, and were shown his stall. They made Lad as comfortable as possible on the straw-littered, raised cage. On one side was a snobbish, gray-streaked collie, whose coloring was called "merle." On the other side was a six-month-old puppy that howled in fright.

The Master paused for a moment in his search for water for Lad, and stared open-mouthed at the merle collie. "Good Lord!" he mumbled, touching The Mistress's arm and pointing to the dog. "That's the most magnificent collie I ever set eyes on. Say goodbye to poor old Laddie's hopes if he competes in any of the same classes with that marvel."

"I won't say goodbye," refused The Mistress. "I won't do anything of the sort. Lad's every bit as beautiful as that dog. Every single bit."

"But not from the judge's view," said The Master. "This merle's a gem. Where in blazes did he come from, I wonder? These out-of-town shows don't attract the Kennel Club stars. Yet this dog is as perfect as Gray Mist ever was. It's a pleasure to see him. Or," he corrected himself, "it would be, if he wasn't pitted against dear old Lad."

He stooped down and patted Lad's satin head. "I'd rather be kicked than take Lad to a show where he'll be beaten. Lad will be sure to know. He knows everything. Laddie, old friend, I'm sorry. Dead sorry."

Then The Mistress and The Master made their way along the collie section, trying to be interested in the line of barking entries.

"Twenty-one collies in all," summed up The Master, as they reached the end. "Some quality dogs among them, too. But not one who has a chance of beating Lad. Not one— except the merle. Lad is due for his first defeat. Well, it'll be a fair one. That's one comfort."

"It doesn't comfort me at all," returned The Mistress. Then she exclaimed, "Look! There is the trophy table. Let's go over. Perhaps the Gold Cup is there—if it isn't too precious to leave out in the open."

The Gold Cup was there. Its presence had already drawn a number of admirers. Sitting behind the table, the village policeman stared at these people with sour distrust. The Gold Cup was a huge metal bowl, its softly glowing surface marred only by the words: MAURY SPECIALTY GOLD CUP—AWARDED TO—There could be no doubt that the trophy was eighteen-karat gold. Its value spoke for itself. The vessel was shaped like a half melon and was supported by four plain claws. Its rim flared outward in a wide curve.

"It—it looks like an upside down derby hat!" exclaimed The Mistress, after one long look at it. "And it's every bit as big as a derby hat. Did you ever see anything so ugly and flashy? Why, it must have cost—it must have cost—"

"Just $1,600, ma'am," said the policeman, beginning to take pride in guarding such a treasure. "$1,600, flat. I heard Mr. Glure say so myself. Don't go handlin' it, please."

"Handling it?" repeated The Mistress. "I'd as soon think of handling the National Debt!"

The superintendent of the show strolled up and greeted The Mistress and The Master. "I see you've entered Lad for the Gold Cup," said the superintendent. "Sixteen collies are entered for it. The conditions for the Gold Cup contest weren't printed until too late to mail them. So I'm handing out the slips this morning. Mr. Glure took charge of their printing. And I don't mind telling you they're causing a lot of fuss. Here's one of the copies. Look it over, and see what Lad's up against."

"Who's the Honorable Hugh Lester Maury of New York?" suddenly demanded The Master. "The man who donated that—that—upside-down gold hat?"

"Gold hat!" echoed the superintendent, with a chuckle. "Gold hat! Now you say so, I can't make it look like anything else. An upside-down derby—"

"Who's Maury?" insisted The Master.

"He's the Man of Mystery," replied the superintendent. "I wanted to get in touch with him about the delayed set of conditions. I looked him up. That is, I tried to. The prize list says he's a New Yorker. But his name isn't in the New York City telephone book. Isn't it funny that he can afford to give a $1,600 cup for charity, but isn't listed in any directory? I asked Glure about him. That's all the good it did me."

"You don't mean—?" began The Mistress, excitedly.

"I don't mean anything," said the superintendent. "I'm paid to take charge of this show. It's no business of mine if—"

"If Mr. Glure chooses to invent Hugh Lester Maury and make him give a gold hat for a collie prize?" suggested The Mistress. "But—"

"That's not what I said," denied the superintendent. "And it's none of my business, anyhow. Here's—"

"But why should Mr. Glure do such a thing?" asked The Mistress. "I never heard of his shrinking behind another name when he wanted to spend money—"

"Here's the list of conditions list for the Maury Specialty Cup," interrupted the superintendent, as he handed The Mistress a pink slip of paper. "Look it over."

The Mistress took the slip and read aloud, "Conditions of Contest for Hugh Lester Maury Gold Cup. First, no collie shall be eligible that has not already taken at least one blue ribbon at a licensed American or British Kennel Club Show."

"That single clause barred eleven of the sixteen entrants," commented the superintendent. "You see, most of these dogs are pets, and hardly any of them have been to any

A.K.C. shows. The few that have, seldom got a blue."

"Lad did!" exclaimed The Mistress joyfully. "He took two blues at the Garden last year."

"I know," said the superintendent. "But read the rest."

"Second," read The Mistress. "Each contestant must have a certified five-generation pedigree, containing the names of at least ten champions."

With relief, The Mistress explained, "Lad had twelve in his pedigree. And it's certified."

"Two more entrants were ruled out by that clause," remarked the superintendent. "That left only three out of the original sixteen. Now go ahead with the clause that puts poor old Lad and one other out of the running. I'm sorry."

"Third," The Mistress read. "Each contestant must go successfully through the maneuvers prescribed by the Kirkaldie Association, Inc., of Great Britain, for its Working Sheepdog Trials."

This time The Mistress protested, "But Lad isn't a working sheepdog! Why, this is some kind of a joke! I never heard of such a thing, even in a specialty show!"

"No," agreed the superintendent, "nor anybody else. A working dog is almost never a show dog. I know of only one either here or in England, and he's an exception, a miracle. So much so, that he's famous all over the dog world."

"Do you mean Champion Lochinvar III?" asked The Mistress. "The dog the Duke of Hereford used to own?"

"That's the dog. The only—"

"We read about him in Collie Magazine," said The Mistress. "His picture was there, too. He was sent to Scotland when he was a puppy, the article said, and trained to herd sheep before he was shown. His owner was trying to get other collie fans to make their dogs useful and not just show exhibits. Lochinvar is an international champion, too, isn't he?"

The superintendent nodded.

"If the Duke of Hereford lived in New Jersey," suggested The Mistress, "Lochinvar might have a chance to win a nice gold hat."

"But he has," replied the superintendent. "He has every chance—in fact, the only chance."

"Who has?" asked The Mistress, puzzled.

"Champion Lochinvar III," was the answer. "Glure bought him. Paid $7,000 for him. The dog arrived last week. He's here. A big gray merle. You ought to look him over. He's a wonder. He—"

"Oh!" exploded The Mistress. "You can't mean it. You can't! Why, it's the most—the most—unsportsmanlike thing I ever heard of in my life! Do you mean to tell me Mr. Glure put up this $1,600 cup and then sent for the only dog that could fulfill the trophy's conditions? It's unbelievable!"

"It's Glure," replied the superintendent. "Which amounts to the same thing."

"Yes!" The Master spoke up harshly. "Yes, it's Glure, and it's unbelievable! And it's worse than that. Don't you see the rottenness of it all? Half the world is starving or sick or wounded. The other half is working its fingers off to help the Red Cross make Europe a little less like hell." The Master continued angrily, "And when every cent counts toward saving lives, this—this Wall Street farmer spends 1,600 precious dollars to buy himself a gold hat. And he does it in the holy name of charity! It's not just unsportsmanlike. It's—it's an unpardonable sin! And I don't want to endorse it by staying here. Let's get Lad and go home."

"I wish to heaven we could!" cried The Mistress. "I'd do it in a minute if we were able to. I feel we're insulting loyal old Lad by making him take part in all this. But we can't go. Don't you see? Mr. Glure is unsportsmanlike. But that's no reason we should be. You've told me, again and again, that no true sportsman will back out of a contest just because he finds he has no chance of winning it."

"She's right," agreed the superintendent. "You've entered the dog for the contest, and by all the rules he'll have to stay in it. Too bad that Lad doesn't know the first thing about working. Neither does the only other local dog not excluded by those rules. And Lochinvar is perfect at sheep work. So Lad and the other dog are sure to make him seem even better. It's awfully bad luck, but—"

"All right! All right!" growled The Master. "We'll go through with it. Does anyone know the rules for working sheepdog trials?'

"Glure does," said the superintendent. "He has the full set of rules in his library. That's probably where he got the idea. I went to him for them this morning, and he let me copy them. The tasks are simple for a trained working dog, but impossible for a dog that is not. Here, I'll read them over to you."

He fished out a folded sheet of paper and read aloud from it. "Guided only by voice and by signs, the dog shall go alone from the center post to the post numbered '1.' He shall go from there, in the order named, to Posts 2, 3 and 4, without returning to within fifteen feet of the central post until he shall have reached Post 4.

Speed and form shall count as seventy points in these trials. Thirty points shall be added to the score of any dog that makes the tour of the posts directed only by signs and without the guidance of voice."

Then the superintendent added, "I was talking to the English trainer that Glure bought along with the dog. The trainer tells me Lochinvar can go through those maneuvers and a hundred harder ones without a word being spoken. He works entirely by signals. He watches the trainer's hand. Where the hand points, he goes. A snap of the fingers stops him. Then he looks back for the next signal. The trainer says it's a pleasure to watch him."

"The pleasure is all his," grumbled The Master. "Poor, poor Lad! He'll get confused and unhappy. He'll want to do whatever we tell him to, but he won't understand. He can't—"

"Hello, people!" boomed a friendly voice. "Welcome to The Towers!"

A large, round-faced person was approaching. He was dressed for the occasion in an outfit that suggested a cross between a stable hand and a minister. Mr. Glure was always dressed for the occasion.

"Hello, people!" repeated the Wall Street farmer, enthusiastically shaking hands with The Mistress and The Master, who did not return his enthusiasm. "I see you've been admiring the Maury Trophy. Magnificent, eh? Oh, Maury's a prince, I tell you! A prince! We think everything of him on The Street. Have you seen my new dog? Oh, you must go and take a look at Lochinvar! I'm entering him for the Maury Trophy, you know."

"Yes," agreed The Master coldly, as Mr. Glure paused to catch his breath. "I know."

The Master abruptly left his cheerful host, and guided The Mistress back to the collie section. There they came upon an angry scene. Unhappy owners were loudly denouncing the Maury conditions list. And they redoubled their complaints upon seeing the two new victims of the trick. People who had bathed and brushed their pets for days, as they eagerly awaited the contest, now glared in hatred at the glorious merle collie. They read the pink slips over and over, with more rage at each reading. One pretty girl sat down on the edge of a bench, gathered her beloved gold and white collie's head in her lap, and cried, unashamed.

The Master glanced at her. Then he swore softly, and set to work helping The Mistress fluff Lad's glossy coat. Neither of them spoke. There was nothing to say. But Lad realized that both his gods were terribly unhappy, and his great heart longed to comfort them.

"Contestants for the Maury Trophy all out!" yelled an attendant at the end of the section.

The Master handed Lad's leash to The Mistress. "Unless you'd rather have me take him in?" he whispered. "I hate to think of your handling a loser."

"I'd rather take Lad to defeat than any other dog to a gold hat," she answered. "Come along, Laddie!"

Naturally, the Maury contest could not be decided in the regular show ring. For this special event, Mr. Glure had set aside a square of lawn, bounded by four white, numbered posts, with a larger white post in its center. A crowd of people was already standing deep on all four sides of the enclosure when The Mistress arrived. The collie judge, who was standing by the central post, stated the rules. Then he asked for the first entrant.

It was the only other local dog besides Lad that had survived the first two conditions. It also happened to be the dog over which the pretty girl had been crying. The girl's eyes were still red as she led her little gold and white collie into the ring. She was wearing a filmy white dress with gold ribbons, which matched her dog's coloring. She looked very sweet and dainty—and heartsick.

At the central post, the girl glanced up hopelessly at the judge standing beside her. The judge nodded toward Post Number 1. The girl blinked at the distant post, then at her collie, after which she pointed to the post. "Run on over there, Mac!" she pleaded. "That's a good boy!"

The little collie wagged his tail, peered expectantly at her, and barked. But he did not move. He did not have the faintest idea what she wanted him to do, although he would have been glad to do it—that is why he barked. After several more useless attempts, the girl led her collie out of the enclosure, almost sobbing as she went. Once again, The Master swore softly.

Now, at the judge's command, The Mistress led Lad into the square and up to the central post. The Mistress was very pale, but her nerves were steady. She, like Lad, was the type that goes down fighting. Lad walked majestically beside her, his eyes dark with sorrow over his goddess's unhappiness, which he longed to lighten. As he moved along with her to the post, Lad thrust his nose lovingly into The Mistress's hand and whined under his breath.

Standing beside the judge, The Mistress took off Lad's leash and collar. Stroking the dog's head, she pointed to Post Number 1. "Over there," she told him.

Lad looked at her doubtfully, and then at the post. He did not see the connection, nor know what he was expected to do. So he looked again at the sorrowing face bent over him.

"Lad!" said The Mistress gently, pointing once more to the post. "Go!"

Now, every dog at The Place knew from puppyhood the meaning of the word "Go!" coupled with the pointing of a finger. Fingers had pointed, hundreds of times, to kennels or open doorways or car seats or whatever spot the dog was supposed to take himself. And the word "Go!" had always accompanied the motion.

Lad still did not see why he was to go where the finger pointed. There was nothing interesting over here—no one to attack, no room to enter. But he went. He walked for about fifty feet. Then he turned and looked back.

"Go on!" called the voice that was his beloved Law. So on he went. He went without questioning because The Mistress told him to. The knowledge of her mysterious sadness made him even more eager to please her.

Soon, as he walked alongside a white post, he heard The Mistress call again. He wheeled and started toward her at a run. Then he halted again, almost in midair, when her hand went up in front of her, palm forward. He'd learned this gesture meant "Stop!" when, as a puppy, he had tried to run into the house with muddy feet.

Lad stood, uncertain. Now The Mistress was pointing another way and calling, "Go on! Lad! Go on!" Confused, the dog started in the new direction. He went slowly. Once or twice he stopped and looked back at The Mistress. But each time came the steady-voiced order, "Go on! Lad! Go on!"

On plodded Lad. He was beginning to hate this new game, which was played without known rules and in the presence of a crowd. Lad hated a crowd. But it was The Mistress's order. And Lad's sensitive ears heard in her voice what no human could hear—a hard-fought struggle not to cry. It seemed all he could do to ease her sorrow was to obey her as best as he could.

Lad continued his unwilling march as far as another post, when the welcome word of recall came. With a bound he started back to his Mistress. But for the second time, he saw that palm-forward signal and heard the cry of "Stop! Go back!" Lad paused and stood panting. This thing was getting on his nerves. And nervousness always made him pant.

The Mistress pointed in still another direction. Now she was calling almost pleadingly, "Go on, Lad! Go on!"

Her pointing hand waved him ahead. So, as before, he followed its guidance. Walking heavily, more and more confused, Lad obeyed. This time he did not stop to look to The Mistress for instructions. From the new forcefulness of The Mistress's gesture, he thought she was ordering him off the field in disgrace, just as he had seen puppies ordered from the house. Head and tail down, he went.

But as he passed by the third of those silly posts, The Mistress recalled him. Happy to know he was no longer in disgrace, he galloped toward her, only to be halted again by that sharp gesture and sharper command. The Mistress was pointing again, more urgently than ever, and in still another direction. Now her voice had a quiver to it—a quiver that even humans could detect. "Go on, Lad! Go on!"

Totally bewildered by his Mistress's crazy mood and the sharpness in her voice, Lad moved away at a disappointed walk, thinking she was again ordering him away. He stopped and looked back at her four times, asking forgiveness for the unknown mistake he'd apparently made. But he was always met by the same fierce "Go on!" So on he went.

All of a sudden, from along the crowded edges of the square, came tremendous applause, punctuated by cries of "Good boy! Good old

Laddie! He did it!" And through the uproar came The Mistress's call of "Laddie! Here, Lad!"

In doubt, Lad turned to face her. He started toward her, expecting at every step that hateful command of "Go back!" But this time she did not send him back. Instead, she ran forward to meet him. A trembling smile had swept the sorrow from her face. The Mistress threw herself down on her knees beside Lad, gathered his head in her arms, and told him what a wonderful dog he was and how proud she was of him.

All Lad had done was to obey orders. Yet, for some unexplained reason, he had made The Mistress wildly happy. And that was enough for Lad. Forgetful of the crowd, he licked at her hands in puppy-like delight.

"Laddie!" The Mistress was whispering to him. "Laddie! You did it, old friend. You did it badly, I suppose, and of course we'll lose. But at least we'll lose right. We finished the contest. You did it!"

By now a lot of noisy humans had invaded the square, wanting to pat Lad and praise him. The Wall Street farmer elbowed his way through the crowd to The Mistress. "Well, well!" he boomed. "I must compliment you on Lad! A really intelligent dog. I was surprised. I didn't think any dog could make the round unless he'd been trained to it. Quite a dog!" Then he added, "But, of course, you had to call to him a good many times. And you were signaling pretty steadily every second. Those things count heavily against you, you know. In fact, they wipe out your chances if another entrant can go the round without so much coaching. Now my dog, Lochinvar, needs only one slight signal for each maneuver. Still, Lad did very nicely. He—" The Wall Street farmer reached out his hand toward Lad. "Why does the mean brute pull away when I try to pet him?"

"Perhaps he didn't catch your name," suggested The Mistress.

She and The Master led Lad back to his stall, where the local people made a fuss over him. Then The Mistress returned to the square. The crowd was thicker than ever, for Lochinvar III was about to compete for the Maury Trophy.

The Wall Street farmer and the English trainer had delayed the event for several minutes while they went through a heated dispute. As The Mistress approached, she heard Glure end the argument by booming, "I tell you that's all rot. Why shouldn't he perform for me just as well as he'd perform for you? I'm his Master, ain't I?"

"No, sir," replied the trainer, glumly. "Only his owner."

"I've had him a whole week," declared the Wall Street farmer. "And I've put him through those rounds a dozen times. He knows me, and he goes through it all like clockwork for me. Here! Give me his leash!" The Wall Street farmer snatched the leather cord from the trainer and, with a yank at it, started with Lochinvar toward the central post. The proud merle reacted to the tug by flashing his teeth. Then the dog thought better of the matter, swallowed his anger, and paced along beside his visibly proud owner.

A murmur of admiration went through the crowd at the sight of Lochinvar as he moved forward. The dog was a joy to watch. It's rare to see such a magnificent dog more than once or twice in a lifetime. Proudly perfect in the way he carried himself, Lochinvar III made people catch their breath and stare. Even The Mistress's heart went out, though with shame for disloyalty to Lad.

Upon reaching the central post, the Wall Street farmer unsnapped the leash. With one hand on the merle's head and the other holding a half-smoked cigar, he smiled upon the tense onlookers. This was his moment. This was the supreme moment that had cost him nearly $10,000. At last, he was sure to win a trophy that would be the talk of the sporting universe. He thought about all the lesser prizes he'd lost to those simple country folk. How they would stare, after this, at his gunroom treasures!

"Ready, Mr. Glure?" asked the Judge.

"All ready!" answered the Wall Street farmer.

He took a pull at his thick cigar. Then, holding it between the first two fingers of his right hand, the dog owner pointed to the first post. No word of command was given. Yet Lochinvar moved off directly in the line laid out by his owner's signal.

As the merle came alongside the post, the Wall Street farmer snapped his fingers. Instantly, Lochinvar dropped to a halt and stood motionless, looking back for the next signal. But the Wall Street farmer had forgotten about his lit cigar. So when he snapped his fingers, the red-hot tip bit deep into his hand. With a loud snort, the Wall Street farmer dropped the cigar butt and shook his hand up and down. This was the gesture that Lochinvar saw as he turned to catch the signal for his next move.

Now, the shaking of the hand and arm, accompanied by a mouthful of curses, is no signal that a working collie knows. Neither is the insertion of two burned fingers into the signaler's mouth, which was the second motion the merle noticed. The dog stood puzzled, not understanding either of these strange signals.

When the Wall Street farmer finally recovered from his childish outburst, he motioned his dog to go on to the next post. But the merle did not move. Here, at last, was a signal he understood. Yet he had been trained to finish carrying out one order before paying attention to the next.

He had received the signal to go in one direction. He had obeyed. He had then received the familiar signal to halt and await instructions. Again, he had obeyed. Next, he had received a wildly emphatic series of signals whose meaning he could not read. But until he understood and followed those commands, he could not go on to the next post. For this reason, the merle stood still.

The Wall Street farmer pointed again toward the next post. Not understanding the earlier signals, Lochinvar watched him for more information. The Wall Street farmer pointed a third time, which only deepened the dog's questioning look. Lochinvar was standing by his hard-learned lessons.

Someone in the crowd giggled. Someone else sang out delightedly, "Lad wins!"

The Wall Street farmer heard. And he began to lose his temper. Once again, these country folk seemed about to take from him a prize he believed he deserved. "You mongrel cur!" he bellowed. "Get along there!"

These words meant nothing to Lochinvar. But the tone told him that his owner had lost his temper—and with it, his authority.

Glure saw red. He rushed across the square, grabbed the beautiful merle by the scruff of the neck, and kicked him. Now, here was something the dog could easily understand. This loud-mouthed giant was daring to lay violent hands on him, the noble Champion Lochinvar III.

As an angry growl went up from the onlookers, a far more murderous growl went up from Lochinvar's furry throat. In a flash, the merle had broken free from his owner's grip. And in practically the same motion, his fangs were burying themselves deep in the Wall Street farmer's leg.

The trainer and the judge rushed over to break up the fight. What the outraged trainer yelled at Glure would have caused a bartender to blush.

What the judge said was, "Mr. Glure, you have forfeited the match by moving more than three feet from the central post. But your dog had already lost it by refusing to work at your command. Lad wins the Maury Trophy."

So it was that the gold hat, as well as the modest little silver Best Collie Cup, went to The Place that night. The Master set the golden monstrosity on the trophy shelf, looked at it for a moment, and then said, "That gold hat is even bigger than it looks. It is big enough to hold a thousand yards of surgical dressings, and gallons of medicine and soup. And that's what it is going to hold. Tomorrow I'll send it to Red Cross Headquarters."

"Good!" agreed The Mistress. "Oh, good! Send it in Lad's name."

"I shall. I'll tell the director how it was won, and I'll ask him to have it melted down to buy hospital supplies. I'll get you something to take its place, as a trophy."

But there was no need to redeem that promise. A week later, a tiny, scarlet, enamel cross came from Headquarters. Its silver back bore the inscription: TO SUNNYBANK LAD—IN MEMORY OF A GENEROUS GIFT TO HUMANITY.

"Its face value is probably fifty cents, Lad, dear," said The Mistress, as she hung the scarlet token on the dog's collar. "But its heart value is at least a billion dollars. Besides, you can wear it. And nobody could possibly have worn Mr. Hugh Lester Maury's gold hat. I must write to Mr. Glure and tell him all about it. How tickled he'll be. Won't he, Laddie?"

CHAPTER 9

Speaking of Usefulness

The man huddled in the tree like a sick raccoon. At times he would stick out his thin neck and look around, but more as if he feared rescue than as though he hoped for it. Then, before slumping backward, he would look down and curse. The big dog lay comfortably at the base of the tree, attentively watching the treed man. There was no reason to waste time or energy barking or running around.

The two had remained that way for a full half-hour. And it seemed they might continue to remain that way until Christmas.

Usually there is something humorous about a man treed by a dog. In this situation, though, only the man was comic. The dog was anything but silly. He was a large collie, with massive shoulders and a deep, shaggy chest. His eyes were dark and sorrowful. In short, he was Lad—the official guard of The Place. Today he was serving as jailer to the man he had seen slouching through the underbrush that grew close to The Place's outbuildings.

It was less than an hour ago that the trespasser entered The Place's grounds from the neighboring woods. He moved softly and at an angle as he advanced toward the outbuildings a hundred yards north of the house. In fact, he moved so cleverly and quietly that no human saw or heard him. Even Lad, sprawling half-asleep on the veranda, had not seen him.

But the wind brought Lad news of a stranger on The Place. So the dog rose to his feet, stretched, and trotted quickly away to investigate. Scent and sound taught him which way to go.

Two minutes later, Lad changed his wolf trot to a slow walk, advancing with head lowered, growling softly. He was making straight for a patch of sumac, ten feet in front of him and a hundred feet behind the stables. The stranger hiding in the sumac patch must have known this, for as the great dog drew near, the man turned and ran. At the same instant, Lad charged.

The man had a ten-foot start. He used this advantage to fling himself at a low-forked hickory tree directly in his path. Then, with the speed of a chased cat, he shinned up the rough tree trunk. Lad arrived at the tree barely in time to collect a mouthful of cloth from the climber's left trouser leg. After this, the dog yawned and lay down to guard his prisoner. For half an hour he lay this way, once or twice sniffing at the ragged scrap of trouser cloth between his forepaws. He sniffed the thing as though trying to memorize its scent.

The man did not seek help by shouting. In fact, he didn't seem to want anyone to find him there. Finally, running out of patience, the prisoner pulled out a jackknife, opened its blade, and threw it at the dog. Seeing the man shift positions as he reached for his knife, Lad thought the man might be getting ready to climb down. So the dog rose to his feet. Then, when the thrower's arm went back, Lad quickly sprang to one side. The knife whizzed, harmless, into the sumac patch.

Lad bared his teeth. Then he lay down again, on guard. A minute later he was up with a jump. From the direction of the house came a shrill whistle, followed by a shout of "Lad! Lad!"

It was The Master calling him. The command could not be ignored. Usually it was obeyed eagerly, but now Lad looked worriedly up into the tree. Then, coming to a decision, he galloped away at top speed.

In ten seconds Lad was at the veranda, where
The Master stood talking with a newly arrived
guest. Before The Master could speak to the
dog, Lad rushed up to him, whimpering for his
help. Then the dog ran a few steps toward the
stables, stopped, looked back, and whimpered
again. "What's the matter with him?" asked the
guest, an elderly, overweight man dressed in
sporty clothes. "What ails the silly dog?"

"He's found something," said The Master.
"Something he wants me to come and see. And
he wants me to come in a hurry."

"How do you know?" asked the guest.

"Because I know his language as well as he
knows mine," The Master replied, and hurried
after Lad.

The guest followed more slowly, complaining, "Of all the idiocy! To let a measly dog
drag you out of the shade on a red-hot day like
this, just to look at some dead chipmunk he's
found!"

Without slowing his pace, The Master
replied, "A man can do worse things than
follow a tip his dog gives him."

"Have it your way," grinned the guest.
"Perhaps he may lead us to a treasure cave or to
a damsel in distress."

"Go ahead and laugh at me if you find it
amusing," said The Master.

"Well, I do find it amusing to see a grown man think as much of a dog as you people think of Lad. It's silly."

"My house is the only one within a mile that has never been robbed," The Master replied. "My stable is the only one in the same radius that hasn't been ransacked by thieves. I have Lad to thank for all that. He—"

The dog had darted far ahead. Now he was standing beneath a hickory tree, staring up into it. "He's treed a cat!" laughed the guest. "How exciting! Come out and get sunstroke, folks! Come and see the cat Lad has treed!"

The Master did not answer. There was no cat in the tree. There was nothing visible in the tree. Lad looked apologetically at The Master. Then he began to sniff once more at the scrap of cloth on the ground. The Master picked up the cloth and walked over to the tree. From a jut of bark dangled a shred of the same cloth. The Master patted Lad's head approvingly.

"It was not a cat," he said. "It was a man. See, the rags of—"

"Oh, nonsense!" snorted the guest. "You people are always telling about Lad's wonderful stunts. But that's all the evidence there usually is to it."

"No, Mr. Glure," The Master replied, trying to control his temper. "No. That's not quite all the evidence that we have for bragging about Lad. For instance, you saw with your own eyes when he herded that flock of stampeded prize sheep for you last spring. And you saw when he won the gold cup at the Labor Day dog show. No, there's plenty of evidence that Lad is worthy of respect."

Then, changing the subject, The Master suggested, "Shall we get back to the house? It's fairly cool on the veranda. By the way, why did you ask me to call Lad? You said you wanted to see him."

"Why, here's the idea," explained Glure, as they made their way to the shade of the porch. "It's what I drove over here to talk with you about. I'm making the rounds of this area. And I didn't actually ask to see Lad. I asked if you still had him. I asked because—"

"Oh," apologized The Master. "I thought you wanted to see him."

"No. I simply asked you if you still had him," explained Mr. Glure, "because I hoped you hadn't. I hoped you were more of a patriot."

"Patriot?" echoed The Master, puzzled.

"Yes. That's why I'm making this tour of the countryside. I want to convince dog owners to do their duty. I've just formed a local branch of the Food Conservation League and—"

"It's a fine organization," The Master said, approvingly. "But what do dog owners have—"

"To do with it?" Glure interrupted. "They have nothing to do with it. That's the pity. But they ought to. That's why I volunteered to make this campaign."

"What campaign are you talking about?" asked The Master. "You say it's to convince dog owners to do their duty. But how? We dog owners have raised thousands of dollars this past year by our Red Cross shows and by donating to all sorts of war funds. And the Collie Ambulance Fund has—"

"This is something better than simply giving extra money," broke in Glure. "It is something that involves sacrifice for our country. A sacrifice that may win the war."

"Count me in, then!" The Master said enthusiastically. "Count in all real dog men. What is the sacrifice?"

"It's my own idea," boasted Glure. Then he added, "Of course, it's been suggested by other people in letters to newspapers and all that. But I'm the first to go out and put it into effect."

The Master, eager for his guest to get to the point, said, "Well, then. Shoot!"

"That's the very word!" exclaimed Glure. "That's the very thing I want all of us dog owners to do. To shoot!"

"To what?"

"To shoot. Or poison. Or smother." Warming to his theme, Glure declared, "In short, to get rid of every dog."

The Master's jaw swung open, and his eyes bulged. His face began to turn red.

Glure went on, "You see, neighbor, when war was declared last month, our nation was caught unprepared. So we've all got to pitch in and economize. Every mouthful of food wasted here helps the enemy. We're cutting down on sugar and meat and fat. But for every cent we save on our food, we're throwing away a dollar by feeding our dogs."

As The Master stared in anger and disbelief, Glure continued, "Our dogs are a senseless, costly luxury! They serve no useful purpose. They eat food that belongs to soldiers. First I'm going to persuade my neighbors to get rid of their dogs. Then I'm going to begin a nationwide campaign from California to New York, and from—"

"Hold on!" snapped The Master. "What idiotic thing are you trying to say? How many dog owners do you expect to accept such a crazy idea? Have you talked to any others? Or am I the first?"

"I'm sorry you feel that way," Glure answered, offended. "I had hoped you were more open-minded. But you are just as pig-headed as the rest."

"The rest?" The Master challenged. "Then I'm not the first? I'm glad the others had sense enough to send you packing."

"They were blind animal worshipers, both of them," said Glure. "Just like you. One of them yelled something after me that I sincerely hope I didn't hear right. If I did, I could sue him for slander. The other knucklehead threatened to take a shotgun to me if I didn't get off his land."

The Master sighed. "Well, I guess those two said everything that needed to be said. I'm sorry there's nothing left for me to say or do. Now, I've read a few of those anti-dog letters in the newspapers. But you're the first person I've met in real life who backs such rot."

"If you were a true patriot, you wouldn't call it rot," Glure snapped back.

"But that's what it is," The Master insisted. "You say dogs ought to be destroyed as a patriotic duty because they aren't useful. There's where you're wrong. Dead wrong. I'm not talking about the big kennels where one man keeps a hundred dogs as if they were so many prize hogs. Of course, those same men raised hundreds of dollars for the Red Cross by showing their dogs at Madison Square Garden."

The Master paused, then continued, "No, I'm speaking of the man who keeps one or two dogs, even three, and keeps them as pets. I'm speaking of myself, if you like. Do you know what it costs me per week to feed my dogs?"

"I'm not interested in statistics."

"No, I suppose not. Few fanatics are. Well, I figured it out a few weeks ago, after I read one of those anti-dog letters. The total upkeep of all my dogs costs just under a dollar a week. Barely fifty dollars a year. That's a fact. And—"

"And that fifty dollars," interrupted Glure, "would pay for a soldier's—"

"It would not!" The Master replied, trying to control his temper. "But I can tell you what it would do. I'd have to spend part of the fifty dollars on insurance, which I don't need now, because no stranger dares to sneak up to my house at night. Part of it would go to make up for things stolen around The Place. For instance, in my stable there are five good harnesses, and two or three extra automobile tires. Unless I'm very much mistaken, the best of those would be gone now if Lad hadn't just treed the man who tried to steal them."

"Pshaw!" exploded Glure. "We saw no man there. There was no proof of—"

"There was proof enough for me," continued The Master. "And if Lad hadn't smelled the fellow, one of the other dogs would have. As I told you, mine is the only place that has never been robbed. And this is the only place on our side of the lake where dogs are allowed to run loose for twelve months of the year."

"But—"

"The women of my family are as safe here as if I had a machine gun company on guard. That counts for more than a little peace of mind, back here in the countryside. Our dogs are an asset in every way, not a liability. They're loyal pals, as well as our best safeguard. All in return for table scraps and skim milk and less than a weekly dollar's worth of stale bread and butcher shop bones. What makes you think that getting rid of them would help the war effort?"

"As I said," repeated Glure coldly, "it's clearly your patriotic duty. I came here hoping to—"

"I'm not one to be sentimental," The Master went on. "But on the day your fool law for exterminating dogs goes into effect, there will be little children crying all over the whole world, little children mourning for the gentle, protecting playmates they loved. And there will be a million men and women whose lives have all at once become lonely and empty and miserable."

The Master glared at Glure. "Isn't this war causing enough misery without your adding to it by killing our dogs? For that matter, haven't the army dogs over in Europe been doing enough for mankind to call for a square deal for their stay-at-home brothers and sisters? Haven't they?"

"That's a bunch of sentimental nonsense," declared Glure. "All of it."

"Maybe it is," agreed The Master. "But so are most of the worthwhile things in life, if you reduce them to their lowest terms."

"You know what a fine group of dogs I had," said Glure, starting off on a new tack. "I had a group that cost me more than any other kennel in the state. Grand dogs, too. You remember my wonderful merle, for instance, and—"

"And your rare Prussian sheepdog. Or was it really a common prune-hound?" added The Master, swallowing a grin. "I remember. I remember them all. So what?"

"So no one can accuse me of not practicing what I preach," Glure continued. "I began this campaign by getting rid of every dog I owned."

"Yes," said The Master. "I read all about that last month in the local paper. Distemper had run through your kennel. Instead of spending money on a vet, you tried to doctor the dogs yourself. So they all died. Tough luck. Or perhaps you got rid of them that way on purpose? As your patriotic duty? I'm sorry about the merle. He was—"

"I see there's no use talking to you," sighed Glure in disgust, rising and waddling toward his car. "I'm disappointed, because I'd hoped you were less bone-brained and more patriotic than these yokels round here."

"I'm not," replied The Master. "And I'm glad to say I'm not. Not a bit."

"Then," continued Glure, climbing into the car, "since you feel that way about it, I suppose there's no use asking you to come to the little cattle show I'm organizing the week after next, because that's for the Food Conservation League, too. And since you're so unsupportive of—"

"I'm not unsupportive of the League," said The Master. "Its card is in our kitchen window. We've signed its pledge, and we're boosting it in every way we know how. Except that we're not killing our dogs, which is no part of the League's program, as you know very well. Tell me more about the cattle show."

"It's a neighborhood affair," said Glure moodily. "Just a bunch of home-raised cattle. Cup and ribbon for best of each breed, and the usual ribbons for second and third. Three dollars an entry. Every entrant must have been raised by the exhibitor. Gate admission fifty cents. Red Cross to get the gross proceeds. I've offered the use of my south meadow at Glure Towers just as I did for the specialty dog show. I've put up a hundred dollars toward the running expenses, too. Micklesen's to judge."

"I don't go in for stock raising," said The Master. "My little Alderney heifer is the only head of quality stock I ever bred. I doubt if she is worth taking up there, but I'll be glad to take her if only to swell the competition list. Send me an entry form, please."

As Glure's car chugged away up the drive, Lad trotted gloomily back to the house. He was unhappy. He'd had no trouble at all in catching the scent of the man he had treed. He had followed the trail through undergrowth and woods until it had emerged into the highroad. But there Lad stopped. For he knew the boundaries of The Place, and he also knew that his own authority ended at those boundaries. Beyond them he was not allowed to chase even the most hated intruder. The highroad was a safe haven for thieves.

For that reason, Lad stopped at the road and turned slowly back. His search was ended, but not his anger, nor his memory of the intruder's scent. The man had sneaked onto The Place.

He had gotten away unpunished. These things bothered, and kept bothering, the big dog.

Two weeks later, the little cattle show took place in a pretty setting at Glure Towers. The big meadow on the banks of the Ramapo River was lined on two sides with temporary sheds. The third side was blocked by a grandstand. The river bordered the fourth side. In the field's center was the roped-off judging enclosure, into which the cattle, class by class, were to be led.

Above the pretty country scene brooded The Towers, homestead of Hamilcar Q. Glure, Esquire. Mr. Glure had begun his career in as a country farmer with the goal of beating everybody else in everything. He had gone into livestock heart and soul. But because he knew little about it, he decided to buy prize stock to enter against the home-raised products of his neighbors.

This did not add to his popularity. Nor did it add to his success. The reason for this was that the judges had a way of handing him a ribbon for second or third prize, and then awarding the blue ribbon to some local exhibitor.

After a while, it began to dawn on Glure that his neighbors thought it unsportsmanlike to buy prize stock and exhibit it as one's own. At about the same time, three calves were born to some newly imported prize cows in Glure's two-acre barns. Their births gave Glure his latest idea. No one could deny he had bred these calves himself. They were born on his own place and of his own high-pedigreed cattle. This is why Glure launched the plan for a show of neighborhood home-raised cattle. He finally felt he was coming into his own.

On the morning of the show, The Mistress and The Master drove over to Glure Towers. Lad went with them. He always went with them. Not that Lad had any interest in a cattle show. But he would rather go anywhere with his gods than stay at home without them.

The show was about to begin when they arrived. The Mistress and The Master, with Lad at their heels, started walking across the meadow toward the well-filled grandstand. Several acquaintances in the stand waved to them as they advanced.

Before they had crossed more than half the meadow's area, their host bore down upon them. Mr. Glure was dressed like a cross between a shepherd and a model for a gentlemen's fashion magazine. He had been walking beside a gaudily dressed stable hand, who was leading an enormous Holstein bull toward the judging enclosure. The bull was steered by a five-foot bar, the end snapped to a ring in his nose.

"Hello, good people!" Mr. Glure boomed, shaking The Mistress's right hand and slapping The Master's shoulder. "Glad to see you! You're late. Almost too late for the best part of the show. Before judging begins, I'm having some of my best European stock paraded in the ring. Just for show, you know. Not for a contest. I like to give a treat to these country farmers, who think they know how to breed cattle."

"Oh?" asked The Master, who could think of nothing more clever to say.

"For example, take that bull of mine, Tenebris," proclaimed Glure, with a wave toward the Holstein. "Best ton of livestock that ever stood on four legs. Look how I—" Glure paused in his lecture, for he saw that both The Mistress and The Master were staring, not at the bull, but at the beast's handler. The spectacle of a groom in gaudy uniform, on duty at a cattle show, was almost too much for them.

"You're looking at that boy of mine, hey? Fine chap, isn't he? A faithful boy. Devoted to me. Very devoted. Not like most of these grumpy, independent local hicks. He's a treasure, Winston is. Used to be chief handler for some of the biggest cattle breeders in the East, he tells me. A week or so ago, I happened to meet him on the road, and he asked for a lift. He—"

It was then that Lad disgraced himself. The man in uniform had led the bull to within a few feet of Glure. Now, without growling or other sign of warning, the formerly peaceful dog changed into a murder machine. Over the many cattle odors, Lad had suddenly recognized a scent that spelled deathless hatred. The scent had been proven correct by a single glance at the man in uniform. That was the reason for the mad charge.

In a single mighty leap, Lad cleared the narrowing distance between himself and the advancing handler. The leap sent him hurtling through the air, straight for the man's throat. The slashing jaws missed the man's throat by only half an inch. That they missed it at all was because the man also recognized Lad, and shrank back in terror.

Even before the eighty-pound weight sent the handler sprawling backward to the ground, Lad's slashing jaws had found a new hold in place of the one they had missed. This grip was on the shoulder, into which the fangs sank deeply. The man went down screaming, the dog on top of him.

"Lad!" cried The Mistress, stunned. "Lad!"

Through the rage that misted his brain, the great dog heard. With a choking sound, he surrendered his hold and turned slowly from his prey.

The Master and Glure took a step toward the approaching dog and the fallen man. Then they both sprang back. They would have sprung further except that the roped walls of the show ring checked them. For Tenebris had taken a sudden and active part in the scene.

During his career in Europe, the gigantic Holstein had won three championships. And during those years in Europe, he had gored to death no fewer than three over-confident stable hands. The bull's murderous temper, as well as the dazzling price offered by Glure, had caused his owner to sell him to the Wall Street farmer.

A bull's nose is the tenderest spot of his body. Thus, with a thick bar between him and his handler, Tenebris was harmless enough. But as Lad's weight knocked the handler to the ground, the man let go of that bar.

Freed, Tenebris stood for an instant in confusion. Then he flung his head fiercely to one side to see the cause of the commotion. This motion swung the heavy bar, digging the nose ring into his sensitive nostrils. The pain maddened Tenebris. A final twist of the head, and the bar's weight tore the nose ring free from the nostrils.

Tenebris bellowed in pain. Then he realized he had shaken off the only thing that gave humans control over him. After a furious pawing of the earth, the bull lowered his head. His evil eyes glared around in search of something to kill. It was the sight of this motion that sent The Master and Glure back against the ropes of the show ring. In almost the same motion, The Master caught up his wife and swung her over the top rope, and into the ring. Glure, seeing the action, wasted no time in wriggling through the ropes after them.

Tenebris did not follow. His red eyes saw one thing and one thing only. On the ground, not six feet away, a man rolled and moaned. The man was down. He was helpless. So Tenebris charged. A bull plunging at a nearby object shuts both eyes. So Tenebris, both eyes screwed shut, threw his 2,000-pound body at the stable hand. Head down, horns on a level with the earth, he made his rush.

But from the very first step, he became aware that something was amiss. His charge did not work out the way he had expected. All because something had thrown its weight against the side of the bull's lowered head. Suddenly, a new and unbearable pain was torturing his blood-filled nostrils. Tenebris swerved. Veering to one side, he tossed his head up to clear it of this unseen torment. As a result, the half-lifted horns only grazed the fallen man. The pointed hoofs missed him altogether. At the same moment, the weight was gone from against the bull's head, and the throbbing stab from his nostrils.

Pausing uncertainly, Tenebris opened his eyes and glared around him. A yard or two away, a shaggy dog was rising from a ground, where he had been tossed by the bull's head. Lad had gone to his enemy's defense. For to dogs, all men are gods—even hated men. With a flash of amazing speed, the collie had flown at the bull just in time to grip its torn nostrils and turn away its whirlwind charge.

Now Tenebris shifted his angry glare from the advancing dog to the howling man. The dog could wait. The bull's immediate purpose was to kill the man. He lowered his head again. But before he could launch his enormous bulk into full motion, the dog was between him and his prey.

In one spring, Lad was at the bull's nose. Again, his white teeth slashed the ragged nostrils. Tenebris halted his rush and tried to pin the collie to the ground. But it would have been easier to pin a buzzing hornet. Tenebris thrust at the clinging dog, once more trying to smash Lad against the ground with his forehead and his short horns. But Lad was no longer there. Now he was to the left, his body clear out of danger, and his teeth in the bull's left ear.

A lunge of the bull's head sent Lad rolling over and over. But as soon as he stopped rolling, he was on his feet again. Not only on his feet, but also back to the attack. A sharp nip in the bleeding nostrils stopped still one more charge.

The bull, snorting with rage, suddenly changed his plan of attack. It seemed his first idea had been wrong. The man could wait. It was the dog that must be gotten out of the way. Tenebris wheeled and made a rush at Lad. The collie turned and ran. But he did not run with tail down, as a beaten dog would. Instead, with tail held high, Lad leapt along at top speed, just a stride or two ahead of the pursuing bull. He even looked back encouragingly over his shoulder as he went.

Lad was having a wonderful time. Seldom had he been so riotously happy. All the pent-up mischief in his soul was set free.

The bull's blind charge was short, as a bull's charge always is. When Tenebris opened his eyes, he saw the dog scampering for dear life toward the river. So again Tenebris charged. Three such charges brought both dog and bull to within a hundred feet of the water.

Tenebris was not used to running. By now he was getting winded. He came to a standstill, snorting loudly and pawing up great lumps of sod. But he had not stood this way longer than

a second before Lad was at him. Shaggy coat
bristling, tail wagging, the dog bounded forward.
He set up an ear-splitting fanfare of barking.
Round and round the bull he whirled, nipping
now at ears, now at nose, now at heels. He easily
avoided the awkward kicks and lunges of his
enemy. Then, crouching like a playful puppy, he
waved his tail and challenged the bull to attack.

It was a pretty sight. And it set Tenebris
into motion at once.

The bull probably thought he himself was
doing the driving. But he was not. It was Lad
who chose the direction in which they went.
And he chose it deliberately. Soon the two were
only fifteen feet away from the river. At this
point, the bank shelved, cliff-like, for two or
three yards, down to a wide pool.

Pretending to attack the nose, Lad got
Tenebris to lower his tired head. Then the
collie sprang lightly over the threatening horns
and landed on the bull's broad shoulders.
Scurrying along the heaving back, the dog
nipped Tenebris on the hip, and then dropped
back to the ground.

The insult and the fresh pain combined
to make Tenebris forget his weariness. Beside
himself with rage, he shut both eyes and
launched himself forward. Lad slipped, eel-
like, to one side. Carried by his own blind

momentum, Tenebris shot over the edge of the bank. The bull opened his eyes too late. Half sliding, half scrambling, he crashed down the steep sides of the bank and into the river.

Lad, tongue out, jogged over to the top of the bank. There, he gazed with interest down into the wildly churning pool. Tenebris had gotten to his feet after the dunking, and was floundering around in sticky, soft mud. He was so tightly bogged down that it later took six farm hands to free him.

By now, people were running down the meadow toward the river. Lad hated crowds. So he made a detour around the nearest runners and tried to return to the spot where he had last seen The Mistress and The Master. If he were lucky, he might have another chance to attack the man he had once treed. That would be an ideal climax to a perfect day.

Lad found all the objects of his search standing together. The hysterical stable hand was swaying on his feet, supported by Glure. At the sight of the advancing collie, the bitten man cried aloud in fear and clutched his employer for protection. "Take him away, sir!" the handler babbled in terror. "He'll kill me! He hates me, the ugly, hairy devil! He hates me. He tried to kill me once before! He—"

"Ah!" said The Master. "So he tried to kill you once before, eh? Aren't you mistaken?"

"No, I ain't!" wept the man. "I'd know him in a million! That's why he went for me again today. He remembered me. I seen he did. That's no dog. It's a devil!"

"Mr. Glure," asked The Master, a light dawning, "when this chap applied to you for work, was he wearing grayish tweed trousers? And were they in bad shape?"

"His trousers were in rags," said Glure. "I remember that. He said a savage dog had jumped into the road and gone for him. Why?"

"Those trousers," answered The Master, "weren't entirely unfamiliar to you. You'd seen the missing parts of them on a tree and on the ground near it, at my place. Your treasured stable hand is the thief Lad treed the day you came to see me."

"Nonsense!" fumed Glure. "Why, how absurd! He—"

"I hadn't stolen nothing!" blubbered the man. "I was coming across the woods to a stable to ask for work. And the brute went for me. I had to run up a tree and—"

"And it didn't occur to you to shout for help?" asked The Master. "I was close by. So was Mr. Glure. So was at least one of my men. An honest job hunter needn't have been afraid to shout. A thief would have been afraid to. In fact, a thief was!'

"Get out of here, you!" roared Glure, convinced at last. "You measly, sneaky thief! Get out, or I'll have you jailed! You're an imposter! A panhandler! A—"

The thief waited to hear no more. With a fearful glance to see that Lad was firmly held, the man bolted for the road.

"Thanks for telling me," said Glure. "He might have stolen everything at Glure Towers if I hadn't found out."

"Yes. He might even have stolen more than the cost of keeping our 'useless' Lad," suggested The Master angrily. "For that matter, if it hadn't been for a 'useless' dog, that mad bull's horns, instead of his nostrils, would be red by this time. At least one man would have been killed. Perhaps more. So, after all—"

He stopped. The Mistress was tugging at his sleeve. The Master, in obedience to his wife's signal, stepped aside, to light a cigar.

"I wouldn't say any more, dear, if I were you," The Mistress was whispering. "You see, if it hadn't been for Lad, the bull would never have broken loose in the first place. In another half-hour that fact may dawn on Mr. Glure, if you keep rubbing it in. Let's go over to the grandstand. Come, Lad!"

CHAPTER 10

The Killer

One of the happiest moments in Lad's daily walk with The Mistress and The Master was his dash up Mount Pisgah. This "mount" was little more than a hill. It was treeless, and covered with short grass and weeds. It rose out of the nearby forests in a long and sweeping climb. Whenever Lad neared the hill, he would always dash forward until he finally stopped, panting and excited, at the top. There he awaited his slower-moving human escorts.

One morning in early summer, Lad bounded ahead of The Mistress and The Master, as they drew near to the summit. As usual, the collie rushed forward up the long slope. But before he had gone fifty yards, he came to a stop and stood, staring. His back bristled, and his lips curled back. His keen nostrils told him something was wrong. The shifting breeze had brought to his nose the odor that had stopped him. It was an odor that wakened all sorts of memories far back in Lad's brain, and which he did not care for at all.

Above him was the green hillside. But its surface was no longer empty. Instead, it was dotted with fluffy grayish-white creatures.

Lad had almost reached the lowest group of sheep when he paused. When several of the animals saw him, they lifted their heads from the grass and started fleeing up the hill. The rest of the flock joined them in the silly stampede.

The dog made no move to follow. Instead, he stared after the sheep that swept upward toward the summit. The Mistress and The Master, too, stopped and stared. From over the top of Mount Pisgah appeared a man wearing blue denim overalls. This was Titus Romaine, owner of the hill. Drawn by the noisy patter of his flock's hoofs, he emerged from under a hilltop boulder's shade to learn the cause of their flight.

Now, in all his life, Lad had seen sheep just once before. That had been when Hamilcar Q. Glure had corralled a little herd of his prize Merinos at The Place. When the sheep had broken from the corral, Lad had rounded them up, without injuring or scaring one of them. The memory was not pleasing to Lad, and he wanted nothing more to do with such stupid creatures. Whining a little, he trotted back to where The

Mistress and The Master stood. As they waited, Titus Romaine angrily bore down upon them.

"I've been expectin' something like that!" announced the landowner. "Ever since I turned these critters out here, this mornin'. I ain't surprised a bit. I—"

"What is it you've been expecting, Romaine?" asked The Master. "And how long have you been raising sheep? A sheep here is as rare as—"

"I been expectin' some savage dog would be runnin' 'em," replied the farmer. "Just like I've read they do. An' now I've caught him at it!"

"Caught whom? At what?" asked The Mistress, failing to note the man's angry glower at Lad.

"That big ugly brute of your'n, of course," declared Romaine. "I caught him, red-handed, runnin' my sheep. He—"

"Lad did nothing of the kind," interrupted The Mistress. "The instant he caught sight of them he stopped running. Lad wouldn't hurt anything that is weak and helpless. Your sheep saw him, and they ran away. He didn't follow them an inch."

"I seen what I seen," answered the man. "An' I give you fair warnin'. If any of my sheep is killed, I'll know right where to come to look for the killer."

"If you mean Lad—" began The Master, hotly.

But The Mistress interrupted. "I am glad you have decided to raise sheep, Mr. Romaine. I hope you'll have good luck. And you are wise to watch your sheep so closely. But don't be afraid of Lad harming any of them. He wouldn't—not for anything. I know. Because I know Lad. Come along, Laddie!" she finished, as she turned to go away.

But Titus Romaine stopped her. "I've put a lot of money into this flock of sheep," he declared. "An' I've been readin' up on sheep, too. I've been readin' that the worst enemy to sheep is predatory dogs. An' if that big dog of your'n ain't predatory, then I never seen one that was. So I'm warnin' you, fair."

"If your sheep come to any harm, Mr. Romaine," replied The Mistress, "I'll guarantee Lad will have nothing to do with it."

"An' I'll guarantee to have him shot an' have you folks up in court, if he does," answered Mr. Titus Romaine.

With this friendly exchange, the two groups parted. Romaine returned to his sheep, while The Mistress, Lad at her heels, lured The Master away from the field. The Master was furious.

"Here's where good old Mr. Trouble drops in on us for a nice long visit!" he grumbled, as they began to walk home. "I can see how it is going to turn out. Because a few stray curs have chased or killed sheep, every decent dog is under suspicion as a sheep killer. If one of Romaine's flock gets a scratch on its leg, even from a bramble, Lad will be blamed. And we'll be in the first neighborhood squabble of our lives."

The people at The Place had always lived in peace with their few rural neighbors. Yet barely three days later, Titus Romaine bore down upon The Place, before breakfast, breathing threats and complaining of slaughter. He was waiting on the veranda, talking with the foreman of The Place, when The Master came out. At Titus's heels stood his hired man, a huge and angry-looking person named Parker.

"Well!" cried Romaine, as he caught sight of The Master. "Well, I guessed right! He done it, after all! He done it. We all but caught him, red-handed. Got away with four of my best sheep! Four of 'em. The cur!"

"What are you talking about?" demanded The Master, as The Mistress joined the group.

"'Bout that ugly big dog of your'n!" answered Romaine. "I knew what he'd do, if he got the chance. I knew it when I saw him runnin' my poor sheep last week. I warned you then. An' now he's done it!"

"Done what?" insisted The Master.

"What dog?" asked The Mistress, at the same time. "Are you talking about Lad? If you are—"

"I'm talkin' about your big, brown collie cur!" snorted Titus. "He's gone an' killed four of my best sheep. Did it during the night an' early this mornin'. My man here caught him at the last of 'em, an' drove him off, just as he was finishin' the poor critter. He got away with the rest of 'em."

"Nonsense!" denied The Master. "You're talking rot. Lad wouldn't touch a sheep. And . . ."

"That's what all folks say when their dogs or their children is charged with doin' wrong!" scoffed Romaine. "But this time it won't do no good."

"You say this happened last night?" asked The Mistress.

"Yes, it did. Last night an' early in the mornin', too. Parker, here—"

"But Lad sleeps in the house every night," objected The Mistress. "He sleeps under the piano in the music room. The maid, who dusts the downstairs rooms before breakfast, lets him out when she begins work. So he—"

"Dress it up any way you like!" broke in Romaine. "He was out last night, all right. An' early this morning, too."

"How early?" questioned The Master.

"Five o'clock," volunteered Parker, from behind his employer. "I know, because that's the time I get up. I went out first thing, to open the barnyard gate and drive the sheep to the pasture. And first thing I saw was that big dog growling over a sheep he'd just killed."

Narrowing his eyes, Parker continued, "The dog saw me, and he wiggled out through the barnyard bars the same way he got in. Then I counted the sheep. One was dead, the one he had just killed, and three were gone. We've been looking for their bodies ever since, and we can't find them."

"I suppose Lad swallowed them," put in The Place's foreman. "That makes about as much sense as the rest of the tale. The old dog would no sooner—"

"Do you really mean to say you saw Lad and recognized him in Mr. Titus's barnyard, growling over a sheep he had just killed?" demanded The Mistress.

"I sure do," said Parker. "And I—"

"An' he's ready to go on th' stand an' take oath to it!" added Titus. "Unless you'll pay me the damages out of court. Them sheep cost me exac'ly $12.10 a head, in the Paterson market, one week ago. An' sheep on the hoof has gone up a full forty cents more since then. So you owe me for them four sheep exac'ly—"

"I don't owe you a red cent!" The Master responded. "I hate the law worse than I hate measles. But I'll fight that idiotic claim all the way up to the court of appeals before I'll—"

The Mistress lifted a little silver whistle that hung at her belt and blew it. An instant later, Lad came galloping up from the lake, dripping with water from his morning swim. The great dog's coat shone in the sunshine. Every line of his splendid body was tense. His eyes looked up eagerly into the face of The Mistress. For a whistle call usually involved something important.

"That's the dog!" cried Parker. "That's the one. He's washed off the blood. But that's the one. I would know him anywhere."

The Master bent over Lad, examining the dog's mouth. "Not a trace of blood or of wool!" he announced. "And look how he faces us! If he had anything to be ashamed of—"

"I got a witness to prove he killed my sheep," cut in Romaine. "Since you won't be honest enough to square the case out of court, then the law'll take a tuck in your wallet for you. The law will look after a poor man's interest."

"I'm sorry you lost the sheep," The Master replied. "Mighty sorry. And I'm still sorrier if there is a sheep-killing dog at large in this region. But Lad never—"

"I tell ye, he did!" stormed Titus. "I got proof of it. Proof good enough for any court. An' the court is goin' to see me righted. An' it's goin' to do more. It's goin' to make you shoot that killer, there, too. I know the law. I looked it up. An' the law says if a sheep-killin' dog—"

"Lad is not a sheep-killing dog!" flashed The Mistress.

"That's exac'ly what he is!" snarled Romaine. "An', by law, he'll be shot as such."

"Take your case to the law, then!" said The Master, finally losing his patience. "And take it, and yourself, off my place! Lad doesn't run sheep. But at a word from me, he'll run you two every step of the way to your own woodshed. Now, clear out!"

He and The Mistress watched the two angrily mumbling intruders plod out of sight up the drive. At The Master's side, Lad viewed the accusers' departure with sharp interest. Schooled in reading the human voice, he had listened alertly to The Master's speech of dismissal. And as the dog listened, his teeth had come into view from beneath a curled lip. His eyes had been fixed on Titus with an expression that was not pretty.

"Oh, dear!" sighed The Mistress, as she and her husband turned indoors and made their way toward the breakfast room. "You were right about 'good old Mr. Trouble' dropping in on us. Isn't it horrible? But it makes my blood boil to think of Laddie being accused of such a thing. It's crazy, of course. But—"

"Crazy?" The Master caught her up. "It's the craziest thing I ever heard of. I mean, Romaine's charge that Lad killed four sheep and only left a trace of one of them—why, that, alone, would get his case laughed out of court. A dog doesn't devour a sheep he kills. He doesn't even lug it away. Instead, he just—"

"Perhaps you'd rather describe it after breakfast," suggested The Mistress. "This awful business has already taken away most of my appetite."

The next morning, The Master was called to the telephone.

"This is Maclay," said the voice at the far end.

"Why, hello, Mac!" responded The Master, wondering why his old fishing buddy, and now the village's local justice of the peace, would be calling him up at such an hour. "If you're going to tell me this is a good day for fishing, I'm going to tell you it isn't. So don't try to tempt me into—"

"Hold on!" broke in Maclay. "I'm not calling you up for that. I'm calling up on business—unpleasant business, too."

"What's wrong?" asked The Master.

"I'm hoping Titus Romaine is," said the Justice. "He's just been here with his hired man as witness to make a complaint about your dog Lad. Yes, and to get a court order to have the old fellow shot, too."

"What!" sputtered The Master. "He hasn't actually—"

"That's just what he's done," said Maclay. "He claims Lad killed four of his new sheep night before last, and four more of them this morning or last night. Parker swears he caught Lad standing over the last of the killed sheep both times. It's hard luck, old man, and I feel as bad about it as if it were my own dog. You know how much I like Lad. He's the greatest collie I've ever known. But the law is clear in such—"

"You speak as if you thought Lad was guilty!" said The Master. "You ought to know better than that. He—"

"Parker tells a straight story," answered Maclay, sadly. "And he tells it under oath. He swears he recognized Lad the first time. He says he volunteered to watch in the barnyard last night. But he'd had a hard day's work, and he fell asleep while he was on watch."

The Master listened grimly, as Maclay continued. "Parker says he woke up at dawn to find the whole flock in an uproar, and Lad pinning one of the sheep to the ground. The dog had already killed three. Parker drove him away. Three of the sheep were missing. The one Lad had just downed was dying. And Romaine swears he saw Lad running his sheep last week."

"What did you do about the case?" asked the dazed Master.

"I told them to be at the courtroom at three this afternoon with the bodies of the two dead sheep that aren't missing, and that I'd notify you to be there, too."

"Oh, I'll be there!" snapped The Master. "Don't worry. It was decent of you to make them wait. The whole thing is ridiculous! It—"

"Of course," went on Maclay, "either side can easily appeal any decision I make. That is, any decision regarding damages. But I'm sorry to say that, by the township's new sheep laws, there isn't any appeal from a local justice's decree that a sheep-killing dog must be shot at once. That's what's making me so blue. I'd rather lose a year's pay than have to order old Lad killed."

"You won't have to," declared The Master, although he was beginning to have a sinking feeling in his stomach. "We'll manage to prove him innocent. I'll stake anything you like on that."

"Talk the case over with Dick Colfax, or any other good lawyer, before three o'clock," suggested Maclay. "There may be a legal loophole out of the muddle. I sure do hope there is."

"We're not going to crawl out through any loopholes, Lad and I," returned The Master. "We're going to come through clean. See if we don't!"

Leaving the telephone, he went in search of The Mistress. By now, even more disheartened, he told her the story. "The worst of it is," he finished, "Romaine and Parker seem to have made Maclay believe their fool yarn."

"That's because they, themselves, believe it," said The Mistress. "And because even reasonable men seem lose their commonsense and humanity when they become judges. But you don't think for a moment, do you, that they can persuade Judge Maclay to have Lad shot?" She spoke with a little quiver in her sweet voice, which awakened The Master's fighting spirit.

"The Place is going to be in a state of siege against the entire law and militia of New Jersey," he announced, "before one bullet goes into Lad. You can put your mind to rest on that. But that isn't enough. I also want to clear him of the charges."

"Didn't you say they claim the second lot of sheep were killed during the night or at dawn, just as they said the first were?" asked The Mistress.

"Why, yes. But—"

"Then," said The Mistress, "we can prove Lad's alibi. Marie always lets him out when she comes downstairs to dust these lower rooms. She's never down before six o'clock, and the sun, nowadays, rises long before that. Parker says he saw Lad both times in the early dawn. We can prove, by Marie, that Lad was safe here in the house till long after sunrise."

Her worried frown gave way to a smile. The Master's own dark face cleared.

"Good!" he approved. "I think that cinches it. Marie's been with us for years. Her word is certainly as good as a farmhand's. Even Maclay will have to admit that. Send her in here, won't you?"

When the maid appeared a minute later, The Master began to question her. "You are the first person down here in the mornings, aren't you, Marie?" he began.

"Why, yes, sir," replied the maid, surprised by the question. "Yes, always, except when you get up early to go fishing or when—"

"What time do you get down here in the mornings?" continued The Master.

"Along about six o'clock, sir," said the maid, bridling a bit, as if scenting a criticism of her work hours.

"Not earlier than six?" asked The Master.

"No, sir," said Marie, uncomfortably. "Of course, if that's not early enough, I suppose I could—"

"It's quite early enough," The Master assured her. "There is no complaint about your hours. You always let Lad out as soon as you come into the music room?"

"Yes, sir," she answered. "As soon as I get downstairs. Those were the orders, you remember."

The Master breathed a sigh of relief. The maid did not get downstairs until six. The dog, then, could not get out of the house until that hour. If Parker had seen any dog in Romaine's barnyard at daybreak, it certainly was not Lad. The maid's testimony settled that point.

"Yes, sir," rambled on Marie. She was beginning to take interest in the examination, now that it centered upon Lad. "Yes, sir, Laddie always comes out from under his piano the minute he hears my step in the hall. And he always comes right up to me and wags his tail, and walks over to the front door, right beside me all the way. He knows as much as many a human, that dog does, sir."

Encouraged by The Master's approving nod, the maid continued, "It always seems as if he's welcoming me downstairs, like, and glad to see me. I've really missed him quite bad these past few mornings."

The approving look on The Master's face gave way to a blank stare.

"These past few mornings?" he repeated. "What do you mean?"

"Why," she returned, made nervous once more by the quick change in her questioner's manner. "Ever since those French windows have been left open, sir. Since then, Laddie don't wait for me to let him out. When he wakes up, he just goes out himself. He used to do that last year, too, sir. He—"

"Thanks," muttered The Master, dizzily. "That's all. Thanks."

Left alone, he sat slumped low in his chair, trying to think. He was as convinced as ever of his dog's innocence, but he had staked everything on Marie's testimony. And now, that testimony was worse than worthless. He crankily cursed his own command that the long windows on the ground floor be left open on summer nights. The night air kept it pleasantly cool against the next day's heat. But for this same coolness, a heavy price was now due.

After a while, his daze of disappointment passed, leaving The Master fighting mad. He quickly revised his defense and, with The Mistress's help, prepared for the afternoon's ordeal. He vetoed Maclay's suggestion of hiring a lawyer, and vowed to handle the defense himself. Carefully, he and his wife went over their plans.

Judge Maclay's court was held every day in a room on an upper floor of the village's community hall. The proceedings there were usually casual. Maclay sat at a battered little desk at the room's far end. His clerk used a corner of the same desk to scribble his notes. In front of the desk was a long table with chairs around it. Here, plaintiffs and defendants and prisoners and witnesses and lawyers sat. Several other chairs were arranged along the wall to seat any additional people.

Promptly at three o'clock that afternoon, The Mistress, The Master, and Lad entered the courtroom. Maclay, Romaine, and Parker were already on hand. So were the clerk and the guard, and one or two spectators. In a corner of the room, wrapped in burlap, were huddled the bodies of the two slain sheep.

Lad caught the scent of the victims the instant he set foot in the room, and he sniffed strongly once or twice. Titus Romaine noted this, and he nudged Parker in the ribs to call his attention to it. Then Lad turned aside in disgust from the bumpy burlap bundle. Seeing the judge and recognizing him, the collie wagged his tail in friendly greeting and stepped forward for a pat on the head.

"Lad!" called The Mistress, softly. At the word, the dog paused midway to Maclay's desk and obediently turned back. The guard was drawing up a chair at the table for The Mistress. Lad curled down beside her, and the hearing began.

Romaine repeated his account of the collie's alleged destruction, starting with Lad's first view of the sheep. Parker retold his own story of twice witnessing the killing of sheep by the dog.

The Master did not interrupt either story. However, on later questioning, he forced Romaine to admit he had not actually seen Lad chase the sheep flock that morning on Mount Pisgah. Instead, Parker had simply seen the sheep running, and the dog standing at the foot of the hill looking up at them. Both The Mistress and The Master swore that the dog had made no move to pursue or attack the sheep.

Thus, Lad won one point in the case. But this point was of little value. Even if he had not attacked the flock upon first seeing them, he was accused of later killing eight of them. And Parker was an eyewitness to this.

With a glance of apology at The Mistress, Judge Maclay ordered the sheep carcasses laid on the table for inspection. While Parker arranged the grisly exhibits for the judge's view, Titus Romaine spoke loudly on the value of the murdered sheep and on the brutality of their slaying.

The Master said nothing, but he bent over each of the sheep, carefully studying the throat wounds. At last, he straightened up and broke in on Romaine's funeral oration by saying quietly, "Your Honor, these sheep's throats were not cut by a dog. Neither by Lad nor by any sheep-killing dog. Look for yourself. I've seen dog-killed sheep. The wounds were not at all like these."

"Not killed by a dog, hey?" scoffed Romaine. "I s'pose they was chewed by lightnin', then? Or, maybe they was bit by a mosquiter? Huh!"

"They were not bitten at all," countered The Master. "Nor were they chewed. Look! Those gashes are ragged enough, but they are as straight as if they were made by a machine. If you have ever seen a dog tear at a piece of meat—"

"Rubbish!" grunted Titus. "You talk like a fool! The sheep's throats is torn. Parker seen your cur tear 'em. That's all there is to it. Whether he tore 'em straight or whether he tore 'em crooked don't count in the law. He tore 'em. An' I got a reli'ble witness to prove it."

"Your Honor," said The Master, suddenly. "May I question the witness?"

Maclay nodded. The Master turned to Parker. "Parker," began The Master, "you say it was light enough for you to recognize the sheep-killing dog both mornings in Romaine's barnyard. How near to him did you get?"

Parker thought for a second, then answered, "First time, I ran into the barnyard, and your dog cut and run out of it from the far side when he saw me making for him. That time, I don't think I got within thirty feet of him. But I was near enough to see him plain. And I'd seen him often enough before on the road or in your car, so I knew him, all right."

Turning to Maclay, Parker went on, "And this morning, Judge, I was within five feet of him, or even nearer. I was near enough to hit him with a stick, and kick his ribs as he started away. I saw him then as plain as I see you. And the light was almost good enough to read by, too."

"Oh?" questioned The Master. "If I remember rightly, you told Judge Maclay that you were on watch last night in the cowshed, just alongside the barnyard where the sheep were, and that you fell asleep, and that you woke just in time to see a dog."

"To see your dog," corrected Parker.

"To see a dog growling over a squirming and bleating sheep he had pulled down. How far away was he when you awoke?"

"Just outside the cowshed door. Not six feet from me. I jumped up with the stick and ran out at him and—"

"Were he and the sheep making much noise?"

"Between 'em they was making enough racket to wake a dead man," replied Parker. "What with your dog's snarling and growling, and the poor sheep's bleats. And all the other sheep—"

"Yet you say the dog killed three sheep while you slept there, and carried or dragged their bodies away, and came back again, and probably started a noisy panic in the flock every time. And none of that racket woke you until the fourth sheep was killed?"

"I was real tired," declared Parker. "I'd been mowing for ten hours the day before, and up since five. Mr. Romaine can tell you

I'm a hard man to wake at best. I sleep like the dead."

"That's right!" agreed Titus. "Time an' again, I have to bang at his door an' holler myself hoarse before I can get him to open his eyes."

"You ran out of the shed with your stick," resumed The Master, "and struck the dog before he could get away? And as he turned to run, you kicked him?"

"Yes, sir. That's what I did."

"How hard did you hit him?"

"A pretty good lick," answered Parker, with satisfaction. "Then I—"

"And when you hit him, he slunk away like a whipped cur? I mean, he did not try to attack you?"

"Not him!" asserted Parker. "I guess he was glad enough to get out of reach. He slunk away so fast, I hardly had a chance to land fair on him when I kicked."

"Here is my riding crop," said The Master. "Take it, please, and strike Lad with it just as you struck him, or the sheep-killing dog, with your stick. Hit him exactly as you hit him this morning."

Judge Maclay half-opened his lips to protest. He knew how much the people of The Place loved Lad, and he wondered at this invitation to a farmhand to beat the dog. He glanced at The Mistress. Her face was calm, even a little amused. Evidently, The Master's request did not horrify or surprise her.

Parker's stubby fingers gripped the crop The Master forced into his hand. With true pleasure in inflicting pain, he took a step toward the collie, and swung the weapon with all his strength.

Then, much more quickly, Parker took three steps backward. For at the threat, Lad had leaped to his feet with the speed of a fighting wolf, dodging the crop and launching himself straight for the man's throat. He did not growl; he did not pause. He simply sprang at his attacker with a deadly ferocity that brought a cry from Maclay.

The Master caught the huge dog midway in his flight. "Down, Lad!" he ordered, gently. The collie, obedient to the word, stretched out on the floor at The Mistress's feet. But he kept a watchful and unloving eye on the man who had struck at him.

"It's a bit odd, isn't it," suggested The Master, "that he went for you, like that, just now, when this morning he slunk away from your blow in cringing fear?"

"Why wouldn't he?" growled Parker. "Now his folks are here to back him up and everything. But he was slinky enough when I whaled him this morning."

"Ah!" mused The Master. "You hit a strong blow, Parker. I'll say that. You missed Lad, but you've split the riding crop. And you made a mark on the wooden floor with it. Did you hit as hard as that when you struck the sheep killer this morning?"

"Harder," responded Parker. "I was so mad I—"

"A dog's skin is softer than a pine floor," said The Master. "Your Honor, such a blow would have raised a welt on Lad's flesh an inch high. Would your Honor mind passing your hand over his body and trying to locate such a welt?"

"This is outside the point!" raged Titus Romaine. "You're dodgin' the issue, I tell ye. I—"

"If your Honor please!" insisted The Master.

The judge left his desk and whistled Lad across to him. The dog looked at his Master, doubtfully. The Master nodded. The collie arose and walked over to the waiting judge. Maclay ran a hand through the magnificent tawny coat, from head to haunch, and then along the dog's furry sides. Lad hated to be handled by anyone but The Mistress or The Master. But at a soft word from The Mistress, he stood stock-still and submitted to the inspection.

"I find no welt or any other mark on him," reported the judge.

The Mistress smiled. The whole investigation was along the lines she'd suggested to her husband—lines suggested by her knowledge of Lad.

"Parker," The Master went on, "I'm afraid you didn't hit quite as hard as you thought you did. Or else some other dog is carrying around a big welt on his flesh today. Now, for the kick you say you gave the collie—"

"I won't do that on your bloodthirsty dog!" cried Parker. "Not even if the judge jails me for contempt, I won't. He'd likely kill me!"

"And yet he ran from you, this morning," The Master reminded him. "Well, I won't insist on your kicking Lad. But you say it was a light kick, because he was running away when it landed. I am curious to know just how hard a kick it was. In fact, I'm so curious about it that I am going to offer myself as a substitute for Lad."

The Master pointed at his foot. "My riding boot is a good surface. Will you kindly kick me there, Parker, as nearly as possible with the same force that you kicked the dog?"

"I protest!" shouted Romaine. "This foolishness is—"

"If your Honor please!" appealed The Master sharply, turning from the bewildered Parker to the troubled judge.

Maclay was on his feet to overrule so strange a request. But there was sharp appeal in The Master's eye that made the judge pause. Maclay glanced again at The Mistress. In spite of the prospect of seeing her husband kicked, her face wore a pleased smile. The judge noted, though, that she was stroking Lad's head, and that she was quietly turning that head so that the dog faced Parker.

"Now, then!" said The Master. "Whenever you're ready, Parker! A fellow doesn't get a chance like this every day—a chance to kick someone. And I promise not to go for your throat, as Laddie tried to. Kick away!"

Parker stepped forward. Probably not sorry to attack the man whose dog had tried to bite him, he drew back his booted left foot and kicked out at The Master's thick riding boot.

The kick did not land. Not that The Master dodged or blocked it. He simply stood motionless and grinned. But the courtroom shook with a wild yell. And Parker drew back his left foot in terror, as a great furry shape came whizzing through the air at him.

The sight of the half-delivered kick at his master had exactly the effect on Lad that The

Mistress had foreseen. Almost any good dog will attack a man who tries to strike its owner. And Lad seemed to understand that a kick is more insulting than a blow. Parker's kick at The Master had thrown the dog into a rage. The memory of Parker's blow at himself was like nothing compared to it. It aroused in the collie's heart a blood feud against the man. Just as The Mistress knew it would.

The Mistress's sharp command and The Master's quickly raised arm were barely enough to stop Lad's charge. The collie twisted in their grasp, snarling furiously. His every muscle strained to get at Parker.

"We've had enough of this!" said Maclay, above the noise of Titus Romaine's protests. "This is a court of law, not a dog kennel. I—"

"I beg your Honor's pardon," apologized The Master. "I was only trying to show that Lad is not the kind of dog to let a stranger strike and kick him, as this man claims to have done. I think I have shown, from Lad's own actions, that it was some other dog, if in fact it was a dog, which raided Romaine's barnyard."

"It was your dog!" cried Parker. "Next time I'll be on watch with a shotgun and not a stick. I'll—"

"There ain't going to be no next time," cried Romaine. "Judge, I call on you to order that sheep killer shot—an' to order his master to pay me for th' loss of my eight killed sheep!"

"Your Honor!" protested The Master. "May I ask you to listen to a counterproposition? A proposition which I think will be agreeable to Mr. Romaine, as well as to myself?"

"The only proposition I'll agree to is the shootin' of that cur and payment to me for my sheep!" insisted Romaine.

Maclay waved his hand for order. Then, turning to The Master, he said, "State your proposition."

"I propose," began The Master, "that Lad be paroled, in my custody, for twenty-four hours. I will deposit with the court, here and now, my bond for the sum of one thousand dollars. This sum will be paid to Titus Romaine if any of his sheep is killed by any dog during that space of time."

The strangeness of the proposal made Titus's leathery mouth hang open. Even the judge gasped aloud at its odd terms. Parker looked blank, until, little by little, the meaning of the words sank into his slow mind. Then he chuckled.

"Do I und'stand you to say," demanded Titus Romaine, "that if I'll agree to hold up this case for twenty-four hours, you'll give me one thousan' dollars, cash, for any sheep of mine that gets killed by dogs in that time?"

"That is my proposition," returned The Master. "To cinch it, I'll let you make out the written arrangement, yourself. And I'll give the court a bond for the money, with instructions that the sum be paid to you if you lose one sheep, by dogs, in the next twenty-four hours. In addition, I agree to shoot Lad, myself, if you lose one or more sheep in that time, and in that way. I'll forfeit another thousand if I fail to keep that part of my contract. How about it?"

"I agree!" exclaimed Titus. By this time, Parker's smile threatened to split his broad face.

Maclay saw The Mistress's cheek whiten a little. But she did not appear worried over the possible loss of a thousand dollars, and the far more painful loss of the dog she loved.

After Romaine and Parker had gone, The Master lingered a moment in the courtroom. "I can't make out what you're driving at," Maclay told him. "But it seems to me you have done a mighty foolish thing. To get a thousand dollars, Romaine is capable of searching the whole country for a sheep-killing dog. So is Parker, if only to get Lad shot. Did you see the way Parker looked at Lad as he went out? He hates him."

"Yes," said The Master. "And I saw the way Lad looked at him. Lad will never forget that kick at me. He'll attack Parker for it, even if they meet a year from now. That's why we arranged it. Say, Mac, I want you to do me a big favor. I want you to go fishing with me tonight. Better come over to dinner and be prepared to spend the night. The fishing won't start till about midnight."

"Midnight!" echoed Maclay. "Why, man, nothing but catfish will bite at that hour!"

"You're mistaken," responded The Master. "Much bigger fish than catfish will bite. Much bigger. Take my word for it. My wife and I have it all figured out. I'm not asking you as a judge, but as a friend. I'll need you, Mac. It would be a big favor to me. And if I'm not wrong, it'll be fun for you, too. I'm risking a thousand dollars and my dog on this fishing trip. Won't you risk a night's sleep?"

"Certainly," agreed the judge. "But I don't get your idea at all."

"I'll explain it before we start," promised The Master. "All I want now is for you to commit yourself to the plan. If it fails, you won't lose anything except your sleep. Thanks for saying you'll come."

At a little after ten o'clock that night, the last light in Titus Romaine's farmhouse went out. A few moments later, The Master got up from a rock on Mount Pisgah's summit. He and Maclay had been sitting on it for the past hour. Lad, at their feet, rose expectantly with them.

"Come on, old man," said The Master. "We'll drop down there now. It probably means a long wait for us. But it's better to be too soon than too late, when I've got so much at stake. If we're seen, you can cut and run. Lad and I will cover your retreat and see you aren't recognized. Steady, there, Lad. Keep at heel."

The trio silently made their way down the hill to the farmstead. They crept along the outer fringe of the property until they came opposite the barn. Soon their cautious progress brought them to the edge of the barnyard, and to the rail fence, which surrounded it. There they stopped. A slight stirring came from within the yard, as the drowsy sheep caught the scent of the dog. But after a moment, the yard was quiet again.

"Get that?" whispered The Master to Maclay. "Those sheep are supposed to have been raided by a killer dog for the past two nights. Yet the smell of a dog doesn't even make them bleat. If they had been attacked by a dog, the scent of Lad would have thrown them into a panic."

"I get something else, too," whispered Maclay. "And I'm ashamed I didn't think of it before. Romaine said the dog wriggled into the yard through the bars, and out again the same way. Well, if those bars were wide enough apart for an eighty-pound collie to get through, what would there be to prevent all these sheep from escaping the same way? I'll have a look at those bars before I decide the case. I'm beginning to be glad you and your wife talked me into this adventure."

"And didn't Romaine say that each night the dog dragged three dead sheep through after him, and hid them somewhere?" added The Master. "No man would keep sheep in a pen as open as all that. The entire story is full of holes."

Lad, at a touch from his Master, lay down at the men's feet. And so, for another full hour, the three waited there. The night was overcast. And except for the low drone of distant tree toads and crickets, it was deathly silent. Once in a while, heat lightning played dimly along the western horizon.

"Lucky for us that Romaine doesn't keep a dog!" whispered Maclay. "He'd have raised the alarm before we got within a hundred yards of here. It's—"

A touch on the sleeve from Maclay silenced the whisper. Through the stillness, a door shut very softly, not far away. An instant later, Lad growled and got to his feet, tense and fiercely eager. "He's caught Parker's scent!" whispered The Master. "Now maybe you understand why I made the man try to kick me? Down, Lad! Quiet!"

At the command, Lad dropped to earth again—though he still rumbled deeply in his throat until a touch from The Master's fingers and a repeated "Quiet" silenced him.

The hush of the night was disturbed once more, very faintly. This time it was by the muffled padding of a man's bare feet, drawing closer to the barnyard. When Lad heard it, he made as if to rise. The Master tapped him lightly on the head, and the dog sank to the ground again, quivering with rage.

The clouds had gotten thicker. Only by a dim pulsing of faraway heat lightning could the watchers make out the shadowy outline of a man, moving silently between them and the far side of the yard. But by Lad's almost uncontrollable trembling, they knew who he must be.

The sheep stirred once more. But they were calmed by the mumble of a voice they seemed to know. A minute later, another gleam of lightning revealed the intruder to the two men who crouched behind the fence. He had come out of the yard and was shuffling away.

But now he seemed to have two heads, and his silhouette was wider. The strange figure dimly appeared for a moment, and then vanished.

"See that?" whispered The Master. "He has a sheep slung over his back. Probably with a cloth wrapped around its head to keep it quiet. We will give him twenty seconds' start and then—"

"Good!" babbled Maclay, excitedly. "It's worked out, to a charm! But how in the blazes can we track him through the dark? It's as black as the inside of a cow. And if we show the flashlights—"

"Trust Lad to track him," replied The Master, who had been slipping a leash around the dog's throat. "That's what the old fellow's here for. He has a kick to punish. He would follow Parker through the Sahara desert, if he had to. Come on."

At a word from The Master, Lad sprang to the end of the leash, his mighty head and shoulders straining forward. And thus the trio started the pursuit.

Lad went in a straight line, without swerving an inch. With difficulty, The Master held him to a slow walk. The two men wanted to keep far enough behind Parker to prevent him from hearing them. But Lad's course was so straight that it led them over a hundred obstacles.

For at least two miles, the snail-like progress continued—most of the way through woods. At last, with a gasp, The Master found himself wallowing knee-deep in a bog. Maclay also plunged into the soggy mud. "What's the matter with the dog?" demanded the judge. "He's led us into the Pancake Hollow swamp. Parker never carried a ninety-pound sheep through here."

"Maybe not," puffed The Master. "But he carried it over one of the paths that lead through this marsh. Lad is in too big a hurry to bother about paths. He—"

Fifty feet above them, a lantern shone on a little hill in the middle of the swamp. It seemed to have just been lighted. The men saw it and strode forward at top speed. The third step caused Maclay to stumble over a bump and land, noisily, in a mud pool. As he fell, he swore an oath that rang through the stillness like a shot.

Instantly, the lantern went out. Then there was a crashing among the bushes of the hill.

"After him!" yelled Maclay, struggling to his feet. "He'll escape! And we have no real proof who he is or—"

Still ankle-high in mud, The Master saw it was useless to try to catch a man who was running away along a dry path. There was only one thing left to do. So The Master did it. Loosening the leash from the dog's collar he shouted, "Get him, Laddie! Get him!"

There was a sound like a cavalry regiment galloping through shallow water. That and a strangely joyful growl. And then the collie was gone.

The two men made for the hill as quickly as possible. They had taken out their flashlights, and these now made the progress much swifter and easier. Nevertheless, before The Master set foot on the first bit of firm ground, all hell broke loose above and in front of him. The men heard the yells of a fear-crazed man, the bleats of sheep, and the tearing of underbrush. But most horribly, they heard what sounded like a rabid beast tearing its prey.

It was this sound which put wings on the tired feet of Maclay and The Master, as they dashed up the hill and into the path leading east from it. "Back, Lad!" called The Master, as he ran. "Back! Let him alone!" As he shouted the command, The Master rounded a turn in the wooded path.

Lying on the ground, twisting like a cut snake and desperately trying to guard his throat with his slashed forearm, sprawled Parker. Crouching above him was Lad. The dog's great coat was bristling. His bared teeth glinted white and blood-flecked in the electric light. His eyes were blazing.

"Back!" repeated The Master. "Back here!"

The collie, still shaking all over with the effort of holding back his fury, turned slowly and came over to his Master. There he stood, stonily awaiting further orders.

Maclay was on his knees beside the moaning farmhand, telling him that the dog would do him no more harm. At the same time, the justice made a quick inspection of the man's injuries. "Get up!" he now ordered. "You're not too badly hurt to stand. Your clothes saved you from anything worse than a few ugly cuts. Stop that yowling and get up!"

Parker gradually stopped moaning. After a while, he sat up, nursing his torn forearm and staring around him. He shuddered at the sight of Lad. Then, recognizing Maclay, he broke into violent speech. "Take witness, Judge!" he exclaimed. "I watched the barnyard tonight, and I saw that cur steal another sheep. I followed him. And when he got here, he dropped the sheep and went for me. He—"

"Very bad, Parker!" said Maclay with disgust. "Very bad, indeed. You should have waited and thought up a better lie. But since this is the tale you choose to tell, we'll look about and try to verify it. Where's the sheep you say Lad carried all the way here and then dropped to attack you? I seem to have heard a sheep bleating a few moments ago. Several sheep, in fact. We'll see if we can't find the one Lad stole."

Parker jumped nervously to his feet. "Stay where you are!" Maclay ordered. "We wouldn't ask an injured man to help in our search."

Turning to The Master, Maclay added, "I suppose one of us will have to stand guard over him while the other one hunts up the sheep. Shall I—?"

"Neither of us needs do that," said The Master. "Lad!"

The collie started eagerly forward, and Parker started still more eagerly backward. "Watch him!" commanded The Master. "Watch him!"

Lad understood.

"Keep perfectly still!" The Master warned the prisoner. "Then perhaps he won't go for you. Move, and he surely will. Watch him, Laddie!"

Maclay and The Master left the captive and his guard, and set out on a tour of the hill. It was a desolate spot, far back in the swamp and more than a mile from any road—a place visited not three times a year, except in hunting season. In less than a minute, the sad bleat of a sheep guided the searchers to the left side of the hill. Here they circled around a thick grove of trees until they reached a narrow opening where the branches were flecked with hanks of wool. Squirming through the opening in single file, the investigators found what they were searching for.

In the center of the grove was a small clearing. In this was a crudely made pen about nine feet square. And in the pen were bunched together six sheep. A scared bleat from deeper in the woods told the whereabouts of the sheep Parker had taken from the barnyard that night. The smashed lantern lay on the ground, just outside the enclosure.

"Sheep on the hoof are worth $12.50 each, at the Paterson market," said The Master, as Maclay blinked at the treasure trove. "There must be $75 worth of sheep in that pen. And there would have been three more of them before morning if we hadn't butted in on Parker's overtime work."

Then The Master explained, "To get three sheep at night, it was well worth Parker's while to switch suspicion to Lad by killing a fourth sheep every time, and mangling its throat with a stripping knife. Only he mangled it too neatly. It wasn't ragged enough. That's what first gave me my idea. That, and the way the missing sheep always vanished into thin air. You see, he probably—"

"But," sputtered Maclay, "why four each night?"

"You saw how long it took him to get one of them here," replied The Master. "He didn't dare start till the Romaines were asleep. And he had to be back in time to catch Lad at the slaughter before Titus got out of bed. He wouldn't dare hide them any nearer home, since Titus has been trying to find the sheep for two full days."

The Master went on, "So Parker was probably waiting to get the pen nice and full. Then he'd take a day off to visit his relatives. And he'd round up this tidy bunch of sheep and drive them over to the Ridgewood road, through the woods, and on to the Paterson market. It was a pretty little scheme all around."

"But," insisted Maclay, as they turned back to where Lad still kept guard, "I still think you were taking big chances in gambling $1,000 and your dog's life that Parker would do the same thing again within twenty-four hours. He might have waited a day or two, till—"

"No," contradicted The Master, "that's just what he wouldn't do. You see, I wasn't perfectly sure whether it was Parker or Romaine or both who were mixed up in this. So I set the trap at both ends. If it was Romaine, it was worth $1,000 to him to have more sheep killed within twenty-four hours. If it was Parker, well, that's why I made him try to hit Lad and why I made him try to kick me. The dog went for him both times, and that was enough to make Parker want him killed for his own safety, as well as for revenge."

As the judge listened, The Master continued, "So Parker was certain to arrange another killing within the twenty-four hours, if only to force me to shoot Lad. He couldn't steal or kill sheep by daylight. I picked the only hours he could do it in. If he'd gotten Lad killed, he'd probably have accused another dog so he could swipe the rest of the flock. At least until Romaine decided to do the watching himself."

"It was clever of you," admitted Maclay. "Mighty clever."

"It was my wife who worked it out, you know," The Master reminded him. "I may seem clever, but it's only because of my wife. Come on, Lad! We're going to wind up this evening's fishing trip by paying a surprise visit to dear old Mr. Titus Romaine. I hope the flashlights will hold out long enough for me to get a clear look at his face when he sees us."

CHAPTER 11

Wolf

There was a long shelf in The Master's study, filled with shimmering silver cups. But in those days, there were only three thoroughbred collies on The Place. And two of them had won them all.

Lad was growing old. His reign over The Place was drawing toward a peaceful close. His muzzle was almost snow-white, and his once graceful body was beginning to show the heaviness of age. He could no longer hold his own with younger collies at the local dog shows, where he had once ruled. Bruce "Sunnybank Goldsmith" was six years younger than Lad. And he was flawless in body and disposition. The Place's third collie was Lad's son, Wolf. But Wolf had neither cup nor ribbon to show for his time on earth. Nor would he ever win a prize, not even in the smallest and least exclusive collie show. For Wolf was a collie in name only. Despite the fact that Lad was his father, he had none of the breed's finest physical qualities.

In spite of all this, Wolf was beautiful. His coat was almost as bright and fluffy as any prizewinner's. He had the collie head and tail, but not the collie ears and shoulders. An expert would have noted his short nose and narrow jaw. In fact, Wolf looked more like his wolf ancestors than the thoroughbred collies that won prizes at shows.

Lad was The Mistress's dog. Bruce was The Master's. And Wolf belonged to The Boy. For the first six months of Wolf's life, nobody except The Boy took any special interest in him. Wolf was kept only because his better-formed brothers had died in early puppyhood—and because The Boy, from the start, had loved him.

At six months, it was discovered that Wolf was a natural watchdog, and that he never barked except to give an alarm. A collie is probably the most excitable of all large dogs. The smallest thing will set him barking. But Wolf, The Boy noted, never barked without strong cause. His value as a watchdog gave Wolf a secure position on The Place. Lad was growing old and a little deaf. At night, he slept under the piano in the music room. Bruce was worth too much money to be left outside at night for any clever dog thief to steal. So he slept in the study. Thus, Wolf alone was left on guard at the house. The veranda was his sentry box.

The Place covered twenty-five acres. It ran from the high road down to the lake that bordered it on two sides. On the third side was the forest. Late at night, boating parties often tried to raid the lakeside apple orchard. Now and then, tramps strayed down the drive from the main road. Prowlers, crossing the woods, sometimes tried to use The Place's sloping lawn as a shortcut to the highway below the falls. Wolf had a ready welcome for all of these intruders. The trespasser could choose either a quick retreat, or fangs in the most easily reached part of his body.

The Boy was quite proud of his pet's skill as a watchdog. He was even prouder of Wolf's incredibly sharp intelligence and his perfect obedience. All these things were a sign of the brain he had inherited from Lad. But none of these talents overcame the sad fact that Wolf was not a show dog, and that he looked positively shabby alongside Lad or Bruce. This annoyed The Boy, even while he could not admit to himself that Wolf was anything less than perfect. Slim, graceful, fierce, affectionate, Wolf was The Boy's darling. But all his life, the dog had won nothing, while Lad and Bruce had been winning prize after prize at one local dog show after another.

The Boy was happy about the winning of each trophy. But for days afterward, he paid more attention to Wolf, trying to make up for his pet's lack of prizes. Once or twice The Boy hinted that Wolf might perhaps win something, too, if he were allowed to go to a show. The Master would always laugh, or else he would silently point first to Wolf's head, and then to Lad's. The Boy knew enough about collies to say no more. For even his loving eyes could see the difference between his dog and the two prizewinners.

One July morning, both Lad and Bruce went through an hour of misery. One after the other, both were plunged into a bathtub full of warm water and soapsuds, and scrubbed unmercifully. After this, they were rubbed and brushed for another hour until their coats shone. "What's the idea of dolling up old Laddie like that?" asked The Boy, as he came in for lunch and found The Mistress busy brushing the unhappy dog.

"For the Fourth of July Red Cross Dog Show at Ridgewood tomorrow," answered his mother, looking up.

"But I thought you and Dad said last year he was too old to show anymore," said The Boy.

"This time is different," said The Mistress. "It's a specialty show, and there is a cup offered for the best veteran dog of any recognized breed. So we're getting Lad ready. There can't be any other veteran as splendid as he is."

"No," agreed The Boy, dully. "I suppose not." He went into the dining room, secretly helped himself to a handful of sugar cubes, and walked out to the veranda. Wolf was sprawled half-asleep on the driveway lawn in the sun. The dog's tail began to thump against the grass. Then, as The Boy stood on the veranda edge and snapped his fingers, Wolf got up and started toward him, his slanting eyes half shut, his mouth grinning.

"You know I've got sugar in my pocket as well as if you saw it," said The Boy. "Stop where you are."

The dog stopped dead short, ten feet away.

"Sugar is bad for dogs," The Boy went on. "It does things to their teeth and their digestions. Didn't anybody ever tell you that, Wolfie?"

The young dog's grin grew wider. His eyes closed to glittering slits. He fidgeted a little, his tail wagging fast.

"But I guess a dog's got to have some kind of consolation prize when he can't go to a show," continued The Boy. "Catch!" As he spoke, he suddenly drew a cube of sugar from his pocket and tossed it in the direction of Wolf. Springing high in air, the dog caught the cube as it flew above him and to one side. A second and a third cube were caught as skillfully as the first.

Then The Boy took the fourth and last cube from his pocket. Going down the steps, he put his left hand across Wolf's eyes. With his right hand, he flipped the cube of sugar into a clump of bushes. "Find it!" he commanded, lifting the hand that blindfolded his pet's eyes.

Wolf darted here and there, stopping once or twice to sniff. Then he began to circle the nearer stretch of lawn, nose to the ground. In less than two minutes, he emerged from the bushes, peacefully crunching the sugar cube between his mighty jaws.

"And yet they say you aren't fit to be shown!" exclaimed The Boy, rubbing the dog's ears. "Gee, but I'd give two years' growth if you could have a cup! You deserve one, all right—if only those judges had sense enough to study a collie's brain, and not just the outside of his head!"

Wolf pushed his nose into the cupped palm and whined. From the tone of voice, Wolf knew The Boy was unhappy, and he wanted to help.

The Boy went into the house again and found his parents sitting down to lunch.

Gathering his courage, he asked, "Is there going to be a Novice Class for collies at Ridgewood, Dad?"

"Why, yes," said The Master. "I suppose so. There always is."

"Do they give cups for the Novice Class?" asked The Boy.

"Of course they don't," said The Master. "But the first time we showed Lad, we put him in the Novice Class, and he won the blue ribbon there. So we had to go into the Winners' Class afterward. He got the Winner's Cup, you remember. So, indirectly, the Novice Class won him a cup."

"I see," said The Boy, not at all interested in this bit of ancient history. Then, speaking very fast, he went on, "Well, a ribbon's better than nothing. Dad, will you do me a favor? Will you let me enter Wolfie for the Novice Class tomorrow? I'll pay the fee out of my allowance. Will you, Dad?"

The Master looked at his son in amazement. Then he threw back his head and laughed. The Boy flushed crimson and bit his lips.

"Why, dear!" The Mistress said hurriedly, noticing her son's embarrassment. "You wouldn't want Wolf to go there and be beaten by a lot of dogs that haven't half his brains or prettiness! It wouldn't be fair or kind to Wolf.

He's so clever, he'd know he was beaten. Nearly all dogs do. No, it wouldn't be fair to him."

"There's a Mutt Class among the specials," put in The Master, teasingly. "You might—"

"Wolf's not a mutt!" flashed The Boy. "He's no more of a mutt than Bruce or Lad, or any of the best ones. He has as good blood as all of them."

"I'm sorry, son," interrupted The Master, catching his wife's eye and dropping his joking tone. "I apologize to you and Wolf. He's not a mutt. There's no better blood than his, on both sides. But Mother is right. You'd only be putting him up to be beaten, and you wouldn't like that. He hasn't a single point that isn't bad from a judge's view."

"He has more brains that any dog alive, except Lad!" declared The Boy, sullenly. "That ought to count."

"It ought to," agreed The Mistress. "And I wish it did. If it did, I know he'd win."

"It makes me sick to see a bushel of cups go to dogs that don't know enough to eat their own dinners," snorted The Boy. "I'm not talking about Lad and Bruce. I mean the thoroughbreds that have been bred and raised for appearance, instead of for intelligence. Why, Wolf's the cleverest, and he'll never even have one cup to show for it. He—" Choking

back tears, The Boy began to eat at top speed.
The Master and The Mistress looked at each
other and said nothing. They understood their
son's frustration, as only a dog lover could
understand it. The Mistress reached out and
patted The Boy gently on the shoulder.

Next morning, Lad and Bruce were put into
the back seat of the car soon after breakfast. The
Mistress and The Master and The Boy climbed
in, and the twelve-mile journey to Ridgewood
began. Wolf, left to guard The Place, watched
the departing show-goers until the car turned
out of the gate. Then, with a sigh, he curled
up on the porch mat and prepared for a day of
loneliness.

The Red Cross Dog Show, that Fourth
of July, was a triumph for The Place. Bruce
won ribbon after ribbon in the collie division.
In addition, he easily took Winners, and thus
added another gorgeous silver cup to his
collection. Then the competition for Best Dog
in Show was called. The winners of each breed
were led into the ring. The judges scanned and
handled the group of sixteen dogs for barely
five minutes before awarding the blue ribbon
and the Best Dog Cup to Bruce.

The crowd around the ring's railing
applauded loudly. But they applauded even
more loudly a little later. This was when, after

a brief survey of nine aged thoroughbreds, the judge pointed to Lad, who was standing like a statue at one end of the ring. These nine dogs had all been famed prizewinners in their time. Above all the rest, Lad was judged worthy of the Veteran Cup! There was a haze of happy tears in The Mistress's eyes as she led him from the ring. It seemed a beautiful climax for his grand old life.

"Why don't you roll your car into the ring?" one disgruntled exhibitor demanded of The Mistress. "Maybe you'd win a cup for that, too."

There was a celebration for the two prize-winning dogs when they got home. But by ten o'clock, the house was dark, for everybody was tired from the day's events. Only Wolf, on the veranda, was awake. Wolf vaguely knew the other dogs had done some praiseworthy thing. If for no other reason, he would have known it by the regretful hug The Boy gave him before going to bed. Well, some must win honors and the right to sleep indoors, while others must plod along and sleep outside, whatever the weather. That was life. Being only a dog, Wolf was too wise to complain.

So for two hours, Wolf snoozed in the warm darkness. Then he got up, stretched, and trotted forward for the night's first patrol of the grounds. A few minutes later, he was skirting the edge of the lake, a hundred yards below the house. The night was pitch dark, except for pulses of heat lightning now and then, far to the west. Half a mile out on the lake, two men in an anchored boat were fishing. At the same time, a small skiff was slipping along very slowly, not fifty feet offshore.

Wolf did not give the skiff a second glance. Boats were nothing new to him, nor did they interest him in the least, except when they showed signs of running ashore somewhere along his beat. And this skiff was not headed for land, but was paralleling the shore. It crept along in dead silence. A man sat at the oars, scarcely moving them as he kept his boat in motion.

A dog is surprisingly nearsighted. At three hundred yards' distance, it cannot, by sight, recognize even its master. But at close quarters, even in the darkest night, a dog's vision is far more piercing than a man's. So Wolf was able to see the skiff and its occupant, while the dog himself was invisible. Since the boat was no concern of his, he trotted on to the far end of The Place, where the forest joined the orchard.

On his return tour of the lake edge, Wolf saw the skiff again. It had shifted its direction and was now barely ten feet offshore. The oarsman was staring at the house. Wolf paused, uncertain. The average watchdog would have barked. But Wolf knew the lake was public property. Boats were often rowed this close to shore without intent to trespass. So it was not the skiff that caught Wolf's attention. It was the man's sneaky way of looking at the house.

A pale flare of heat lightning briefly turned the world from jet black to a dim sulfur color. The boatman saw Wolf standing, alert and suspicious, among the lakeside grasses, not ten feet away. He started slightly. And a soft, throaty growl from the dog answered him. The man seemed to take the growl as a challenge, and to accept it. He reached into his pocket and took something out. Then he lifted the thing and threw it at Wolf.

With all the quickness of his wolf ancestors, the dog easily dodged the object, which landed on The Lawn behind him. Teeth bared in a snarl, Wolf dashed forward through the shallow water toward the skiff. But the man seemed to have had enough of this business. He rowed off into deep water. And once there, he kept on rowing until distance and darkness hid him.

Wolf stood, chest-deep in water, listening to the far-off oar strokes until they died away. He was not foolish enough to swim after the boat. He knew that a swimming dog is worse than helpless against a boatman. Moreover, the intruder had been scared away. That was all that concerned Wolf. He turned back to shore. His vigil was ended for another few hours. Now it was time to take up his nap where he had left off. But before he had taken two steps, his sensitive nostrils were full of the scent of raw meat. There, on The Lawn ahead of him, lay a chunk of beef as big as a fist. This, then, was what the boatman had thrown at him!

Wolf pricked up his ears, and his tail began to wag. Trespassers had once or twice tried to stone him, but this was the first time any of them had pelted him with delicious raw beef. Evidently, Lad and Bruce were not the only collies on The Place to receive prizes that day. Wolf stooped over the meat, sniffed at it, then caught it up between his jaws.

Now, a dog is the easiest animal alive to poison, just as a cat is the hardest. While a dog will usually bolt a mouthful of poisoned meat without stopping to chew it, a cat smells and tastes everything first. The slightest unfamiliar scent or flavor warns a cat off the feast. So the average dog would have gulped this tasty treat. But Wolf was not the average dog. No collie is. And Wolf was even more like his wild ancestors than are most collies.

Wolf lacked the reasoning powers to make him suspicious of this rich gift from a stranger. But he was a gourmet. He always took three times as long as the other dogs to eat his dinner. For instead of gobbling his meal, as they did, Wolf tended to nibble at each morsel. This odd little trait now saved Wolf's life.

Wolf carried the lump of beef gingerly up to the veranda, laid it down on his mat, and prepared to enjoy his lucky banquet in his own picky way. Holding the beef between his forepaws, he began to devour it in dainty little bites. About a quarter of the meat had disappeared when Wolf became aware that his tongue hurt and his throat was sore. He also noticed that the inside of the ball of meat had a foul odor. He looked down at the chunk, rolled it over with his nose, examined it again, and then got up and moved away from it in disgust.

Soon he forgot his disappointment when he realized he was very, very ill. His tongue and throat no longer burned, but his body and brain seemed full of hot lead. He felt stupid, and too weak to move. Drowsiness gripped him. With a grunt of discomfort and total exhaustion, he slumped down on the veranda floor to sleep off his sickness. For a while after that, nothing mattered.

For perhaps an hour, Wolf lay there, dead to his duty and to everything else. Then faintly, through the fog of dullness that clouded his brain, came a sound he had long ago learned to listen for. It was the scraping noise of a boat's prow drawn up on the pebbly shore at the foot of The Lawn. Instinct tore through the poison vapors and awakened the sick dog. He lifted his head, which was strangely heavy and hard to lift.

The sound was repeated, as the prow was pulled farther up on the bank. Then came the crunch of a human foot on the waterside grass.

Heredity and training and lifelong loyalty took control of the sluggish dog, dragging him to his feet and down the veranda steps through no will of his own. Every motion tired him. He was dizzy and nauseated. He craved sleep. But unlike a human, he did not stop to think up good reasons why he should not do his duty.

Wolf trotted slowly and shakily to the brow of the hill. His sharp hearing told him the trespasser had left his boat and taken one or two steps up The Lawn toward the house. Then a puff of wind brought Wolf's sense of smell into action. A dog remembers odors as humans remember faces. And the breeze carried to him the scent of the same man who had tossed ashore that bit of meat, which had caused all his suffering.

Having played such a cruel trick on him, the joker actually dared to intrude on The Place! A gust of rage sent a thrill of fierce energy through Wolf. Down the hill he flew, teeth bared, back bristling from neck to tail. Soon he was well within sight of the intruder. He saw the man pause to adjust something on one of his hands. But before the man finished, Wolf saw him stop and stare through the darkness as he heard the wild onrush of the dog's feet.

Another instant and Wolf was near enough to spring. Out of the blackness, the dog launched himself, straight for the trespasser's face. The man saw the dim shape hurtling through the air toward him. He dropped what he was carrying and threw up both hands to guard his neck. He was none too soon. For just as the thief's palm reached his own throat, Wolf's teeth met in the fleshy part of the hand.

Silent, in agony, the man beat at the dog with his free hand. But an attacking collie is hard to locate in the darkness. Wolf's snapping jaws had already deserted the robber's mangled hand and slashed the man's left shoulder to the bone. Then the dog made another furious lunge for the face. The man crashed down, losing his balance under the heavy impact of Wolf. To protect his throat, the man rolled over on his face, kicking madly at the dog. Then he reached back for his hip pocket. Half in the water and half on the bank, the two struggled, the man panting in terror, the dog growling and snarling like a wild animal.

The thief's torn left hand found a grip on Wolf's throat. He shoved the fiercely twisting dog backward, jammed a pistol against Wolf's head, and pulled the trigger! The dog relaxed his grip and tumbled in a heap. The man staggered, gasping, to his feet. He was bleeding, and his clothes were torn and coated with mud.

The sound of the shot was still echoing among the hills when several of the house's dark windows leaped into sudden light. The thief cursed. His night's work was ruined. He bent over his skiff and shoved it into the water. Then he turned to grope for what he had dropped on The Lawn. As he did so, something seized him by the ankle. In panic, the man screamed and jumped into the water. Then, peering back, he saw what had happened. Wolf, sprawling and unable to stand, had reached forward from where he lay and drove his teeth for the last time into his enemy.

The thief raised his pistol again and fired at the dog. Then he crawled into his boat and rowed off with frantic speed, just as a flurry of barks announced that Lad and Bruce had been released from the house. The collies came charging down The Lawn, The Master at their heels. But the quick oar beats were already growing distant, and the gloom had blotted out any chance of seeing or following the boat.

Wolf lay on his side, half in and half out of the water. He could not rise to meet The Boy, who came running up, close behind The Master. But the dog wagged his tail in feeble greeting, then looked out over the black lake and snarled. The bullet had grazed Wolf's scalp and then passed along the foreleg, scarring and numbing it. No damage had been done that a week's nursing would not set right.

The marks in the grass and the poisoned meat on the porch told their own tale. So did the kit of burglar tools and a rubber glove found near the foot of The Lawn. Then the telephone was put to work.

At dawn, a man in torn and muddy clothes called at the office of a doctor three miles away. He asked to be treated for dog bites that he claimed to have received from a pack of stray curs he had met on the road. By the time his wounds were treated, the sheriff and two deputies had arrived to take him into custody. In his pockets were a revolver, with two cartridges fired, and the mate of the rubber glove he had left on The Place's lawn.

"You—you—wouldn't let Wolfie go to any show and win a cup for himself," The Boy half-sobbed, as The Master treated the injured dog's wound. "But he's saved you from losing all the cups the other dogs ever won!"

Three days later, The Master came home from a trip to the city. He went straight to The Boy's room. There on a rug lay Wolf, The Boy sitting beside him, stroking the dog's bandaged head.

"Wolf," said The Master, solemnly, "I've been talking about you to some people I know. And we all agree—"

"Agree what?" asked The Boy, looking up in mild curiosity.

The Master cleared his throat and continued, "We all agree that the trophy shelf in my study doesn't have enough cups on it. So I've decided to add still another to the collection. Want to see it, son?" From behind his back, The Master produced a gleaming silver cup, one of the largest and finest The Boy had ever seen. It was even larger than Bruce's Best Dog Cup.

The Boy took it from his father's hand. "Who won this?" he asked. "And for what? Didn't we get all the cups that were coming to us at the show?"

The Boy's voice trailed away. He had caught sight of the lettering on the big cup. And now, his arm around Wolf, he read the inscription aloud, stammering with delight as he blurted out the words, "SPECIALTY CUP—WON BY WOLF, AGAINST ALL ENTRANTS!"

CHAPTER 12

The Last Great Adventure

For more years than he could remember, Lad had been king. The other dogs at The Place recognized Lad's rule. It would no more have occurred to any of them to pass through a doorway ahead of Lad than it would occur to a nobleman to shoulder his way into the throne room ahead of his king.

Lad was great. And now, at thirteen, he was old—very old. His long, clean lines had become blurred with flesh, as he'd put on weight. He could no longer run as fast or as far as before. A brisk five-mile walk made him eager for an hour's rest.

Even so, Lad was healthy. His spirit and his intelligence had not faltered. He would still dash out of the house, barking wildly when The Mistress or The Master returned home. He would still jump excitedly around either of them at the hint of a walk. But it took effort. And despite Lad's brave attempts at youthfulness, everyone could see he was old.

Lad no longer led the other dogs in their rushes through the forest in search of rabbits. Since he could not keep up, he let the others go on without him. He contented himself with an occasional lone walk through the woods, where he had once led the run.

There had been many dogs at The Place during Lad's reign, dogs of all sorts, including Lad's worshiped collie mate, Lady. But now there were only three dogs beside himself. One of them was Wolf. Lad had trained this son of his and taught him all he knew. The second of the remaining dogs was Bruce, descendant of eleven international champions and winner of many a ribbon and medal and cup.

The third was Rex—a giant, a freak, a dog strangely out of place among a group of thoroughbreds. On his father's side Rex was pure collie, and on his mother's, pure bull terrier. He looked more like a Great Dane than anything else. He was shorthaired, two inches taller and ten pounds heavier than Lad, and had the bunch-muscled jaws of a killer. There was not an outside dog for two miles in either direction that Rex had not met and defeated. The bull terrier strain, when blended with collie blood, made Rex a terrific fighter. He was swift as a deer, and strong as a puma.

In many ways, he was a lovable and affectionate pet—wildly devoted to The Master, and extremely jealous of the latter's love for Lad. Rex was five years old, and in his prime. Like the other dogs, he had always taken Lad's rule for granted.

That year, March was a month of drearily repeated snows. In the forests beyond The Place, the snow lay sixteen inches deep. One snowy, blowy, bitter cold Sunday, Rex and Wolf decided to go rabbit hunting.

The dogs had been lying comfortably in the living room, where a cozy fire was burning. The Mistress was reading; The Master was asleep. But Rex, who had been restless lately, was bored. There seemed no chance that either human would go for a walk. The winter forests were calling. And the warmly quivering body of a new-caught rabbit was a tremendous lure. So Rex got to his feet, went over to Bruce, and touched his nose. The drowsing collie paid no attention.

Next, Rex moved over to where Wolf lay on the old fur rug. The two dogs' noses touched. By that touch, Wolf understood Rex's hint to join him. Wolf was not yet four years old. He was still at an age when excitement outweighs comfort. Moreover, he admired and imitated Rex, as much as the school's littlest boy models himself on the class bully. He was up at once and ready to start.

While a maid was bringing in wood from the veranda, the two dogs slipped out through the half-open door. As they went, Wolf cast a sidelong glance at Lad, who was snoozing under the piano. Lad noted the careless invitation. He also noted that Wolf did not hesitate when his father refused to join the outing, but instead trotted gaily off behind Rex. Perhaps this lack of loyalty hurt Lad's sensitive feelings. Perhaps the two dogs' departure only woke in him the memory of the joys of the chase and stirred a longing for the snowy woods.

For a minute or two, the big living room was quiet. Then Lad got up heavily and walked out of his piano cave. He stretched and crossed to The Mistress's chair. There he sat down very close beside her and laid one of his tiny white forepaws in her lap. Still absorbed in her book, The Mistress put out a hand and patted Lad's ruff and ears.

Lad often came to her or to The Master for petting. After receiving it, he would return to his resting place. But today he was trying to attract her notice for something much more important. It had occurred to him that it would be fun to go with her for a walk in the snow. And since his presence failed to get across this hint, he began to "talk."

Lad talked only to The Mistress and The Master, and then only in moments of stress or appeal. No one hearing him could doubt the dog was trying to frame human speech. This talking would continue sometimes for several minutes without stopping. Its tones carried whatever emotion the old dog was trying to convey.

The Mistress looked up. "What is it, Laddie? What do you want?"

For answer, Lad glanced at the door, and then at The Mistress. Then he went out into the hall. Soon he returned with one of her fur gloves in his mouth.

"No, no," The Mistress laughed. "Not today, Lad. Not in this storm. We'll take a good long walk tomorrow."

The dog sighed and returned sadly to his cave beneath the piano. But the vision of the forests was hard to erase from his mind. So a little later, when the front door was opened again by the maid, he stalked out. The snow was driving hard, and there was a sting in it. The temperature was a little above zero, but the cold was harmless against the woven thickness of Lad's coat. Picking his way along the driveway, he strolled toward the woods. Here, through the drifted undergrowth, Rex and Wolf had recently swept along in pursuit of a rabbit. Even a human eye could not have missed their partly covered tracks. But Lad knew whose track was whose, and which dog had been in the lead.

A partridge rocketed upward through a clump of evergreens, while a weasel glared after it, confused. A crow, its black feet red with a slain snowbird's blood, flapped clumsily overhead. Humans would have described the white-shrouded wilderness as a peaceful place. But Lad knew better. Beneath the surface, Nature is never solitary and never at peace.

When a dog is very old and very heavy, it is hard to walk through sixteen-inch snow, even slowly. As a result, Lad was happy to come upon a narrow woodland track made by a worker who had passed and re-passed through that same strip of forest during the last few hours. To follow in that trampled rut made walking much easier.

Lad rambled along. After a while, his ears and nose told him that his two loving friends, Rex and Wolf, were coming toward him on their way home. Lad's tail wagged. He was growing a bit lonely on this Sunday afternoon walk. It would be a pleasure to have company, especially Wolf's.

Rex and Wolf had done poorly on their hunt. They had chased two rabbits. One rabbit had doubled back and completely escaped them. But in the chase, Rex cut his foot on a strip of unseen barbed wire. And the icy snow had gotten into the jagged cut in a very irritating way. The second rabbit had dived under a log. Rex thrust his head through a snow bank in search of the vanished prey. But a briar thorn plunged its needle point deep into his left nostril. The pain wrung a yell of rage and hurt from the big dog.

With both a nostril and a foot hurt, there was no more fun in hunting. So, angry and in pain, Rex loped homeward, with Wolf pattering along behind him. Like Lad, they came upon the trampled path and took advantage of the easier going.

So it was, at a turn in the track, that they came face-to-face with Lad. Wolf had already smelled him, and his tail began to wag in welcome. Rex, his nose throbbing, could smell nothing. He did not know of Lad's presence until that turn. He halted, annoyed and angry. His wounds brought to a head the strange restlessness that had overtaken him lately. Rex was not himself. His mind was sick.

There was not enough room for two large dogs to pass each other on that narrow trail. One or the other would have to wade out into the deep snow on either side. Ordinarily, there would be no question about which dog on The Place would make way for Lad. It would have been a matter of course. And so, today Lad expected Rex to step out of the rut.

Lad moved onward, until he was less than a yard away from Rex. But Rex, his brain feverish and his wounds torturing him, suddenly rebelled. Without so much as a growl of warning, he threw himself upon Lad, and flew straight at the tired old dog's throat.

Lad was caught completely off guard. One minute he was plodding toward his two supposedly loyal friends. The next minute, Rex's ninety pounds of muscle knocked him down, and the fearsome jaws found a grip in the soft fur of his throat. Down crashed Lad, his snarling enemy upon him, pinning him to the ground, the huge jaws tearing and slashing at his ruff.

Maddened by rage, Rex misjudged his mark, missing the jugular. And since collies are never completely taken by surprise, Lad instinctively threw his body sideways, feet down, to avoid Rex's full impact. With a heave that wrenched every muscle, Lad shook off Rex and scrambled free.

The old collie was free to turn tail and run for his life, but his heroic heart would not let him do this. He was also free to stand his ground and fight until he was killed by his younger, larger, and stronger enemy. But his intelligence would not permit such foolishness. There was one chance and only one—a compromise between sanity and honor. Lad took this chance.

He would not run. He could not save his life by fighting where he stood. His only hope was to keep his face to his enemy, battling as best he could, and all the time keep backing toward home. If he could last until he came within sight or sound of the people at the house, he knew he would be saved. Home was a full half-mile away, and the snow was almost chest deep. Yet he instantly laid out his plan and put it into action.

Just after Lad got to his feet, Rex cleared his mouth of hair and flew again at the old dog. Lad dodged the snapping jaws by an inch, at the same time burying his teeth in the right side of Rex's face. All the while, Lad kept giving ground, moving backward three or four yards, helped along by his opponent's momentum. He could not turn to gauge the direction toward home. Yet he moved at exactly the correct angle.

Lad's hold on Rex's cheek was good, but it was not good enough. At thirteen, a dog's biting teeth are dull, and his fangs are blunted. Nor is the jaw as powerful as it once was. Rex twisted in the fierce grip, and soon tore free and attacked again. Now he was trying to lunge over the top of Lad's lowered head to the nape of the neck, where sharp teeth can pierce through to the spinal cord.

Rex lunged three times. And three times Lad reared on his hind legs, snapping and slashing at his enemy. And between each charge, he went backward a few more steps. By now, they had left the path and were plowing through deep snow. The snow did not slow Rex, but it slowed the steadily backing Lad. Lad's extra flesh, too, was a handicap. He was growing winded and weary.

Under the gray skies and the driving snow, the fight swirled. The great dogs reared, clashed, tore, lost their footing and rolled, staggered up again, and renewed the attack. Always Lad worked his way backward, waging a desperate rear-guard action. In the battle's wake was a line of blood-spattered snow.

It was slow going, this ever-fighting retreat of Lad's, through the deep drifts, with Rex pressing him and tearing at him with every backward step. The old dog's wind was gone.

His once-mighty strength was going. But he fought on with the fury of a dying king who will not be overthrown. Again and again Lad slashed at Rex. But the old dog's slashes had lost their former lightning speed and skill. And the blunt fangs scored only minor cuts in Rex's hide.

There was little hope of reaching home alive. Lad must have known that. His strength was gone. It was his noble heart that was now doing his fighting, not his aged body. Lad had never known the word "quit." That is why he battled on—never turning tail, never dreaming of surrender, taking serious wounds, and inflicting only light ones.

Down went Lad. Then once more he struggled to his feet, and gained another three yards of ground. Rex was upon him with one leap, the bloody jaws striking for the old dog's throat. Lad reared to block the attack. Then suddenly, knocked off balance, he crashed backward into the snowdrift.

But it wasn't Rex who tackled him. It was young Wolf.

If this were a fairy tale, Wolf might have sprung to the aid of his father and saved his life. But the shameful truth is that Wolf did nothing of the kind. Rex was his model, the bully he had so long imitated. Now Rex was fighting a most entertaining battle, and fighting it with a fury that made his young follower eager to share in the glory. That is why, as Lad reared to meet Rex's lunge, Wolf threw himself upon the old dog's flank, burying his white teeth in the muscles of the lower leg. The rear attack bowled Lad completely over. He was thrown upon his back, and both his murderers plunged at his unguarded throat and lower body.

But a collie thrown is not a collie beaten. For thirty seconds or more, the three thrashed about in a growling, snarling, unloving embrace. Then, by some miracle, Lad was on his feet again. The old dog's throat had a new and deep wound, dangerously close to the jugular. His stomach and left side were slashed. But he was up. And even with both dogs flinging themselves upon him, he gained another yard or two in his line of retreat.

Now his attackers started colliding and blocking each other's charges, which might have let Lad gain more ground. But for the first time, Lad's wise old brain clouded and his hero heart went sick, as he saw his own son battling against him. He could not understand. Loyalty was as much a part of him as were his sorrowful brown eyes and his tiny white forepaws. Wolf's amazing treachery seemed to numb the old warrior's body and mind.

But Lad's stunned confusion passed quickly. A righteous anger surged in its place, an anger that brought back youth and strength to the aged fighter. With a yell that echoed far through the forest's silence, Lad whizzed forward at Rex. Wolf, who was nearer, struck for his father's throat, missed, and rolled in the snow. Lad paid no attention to him. Straight for Rex he leaped. Rex, bounding at him, was already in midair. The two met. And under the wild charge, Rex fell back into the snow.

Lad was upon him at once. The worn-down teeth found their goal above the jugular. They plunged deep, driven by the brief flash of power that kept Lad going. That grip almost ended the fight, leaving Rex gasping out his life in the snow. But the false strength faded. Rex, roaring like a hurt tiger, twisted and tore himself free. Lad gave ground, backing away from two attackers instead of one.

It was easier now to retreat. For Wolf, unskilled in warfare, at first hindered Rex almost as much as he helped him. Again and again, he got in the bigger dog's way, spoiling a rush. Had Wolf understood the idea of teamwork sooner, Lad would have been pulled down and slaughtered in less than a minute.

Finally, Wolf grasped the importance of keeping out of Rex's way. And he realized he could do more damage by attacking his enemy from a different angle, instead of lunging alongside his ally. After that, Wolf fought more cleverly. His favorite trick was to dive for Lad's forelegs and try to break them. Several times, Wolf's jaws reached the slender white forelegs, slashing them and throwing Lad off balance. Once he found a hold on the left haunch and held it until his victim shook loose by rolling.

Lad defended himself from this new foe as well as he could. He dodged him, or brushed him to one side. But never once did he attack Wolf, or even snap at him. The old dog fought his way backward—repeatedly brought down to earth, and each time staggering up weaker than before.

The forest was behind them now. The deserted highroad was passed. Under Lad's reeling feet was, at last, the dear ground of The Place—The Place where for thirteen happy years he had ruled his own kind and served his gods. But the house was still almost two hundred yards away, and Lad was nearly dead. His body was one mass of wounds. His strength had turned to water. His breath was gone. His bloodshot eyes were dim. His brain was dizzy, and refused to serve him. Loss of blood had weakened him as much as the tremendous effort of fighting.

Yet Lad continued to fight. It was a terribly useless struggle. The other dogs were all over him. Unhindered by Lad's puny effort to fend them off, they tore, slashed, and gripped at will.

Finally, the time for slaughter had come. Drunk with blood and fury, the attackers plunged at Lad for the last time. Down went Lad, helpless beneath the murderous avalanche that overwhelmed him. And this time, his body flatly refused to obey the grim command of his will. The fight was over—the last, good fight of a pure-hearted hero against hopeless odds.

In the home, the living room fire crackled cheerily. The snow hissed against the glass. At twilight, a sheet of frost on every pane shut out the stormy world. The loud screech of the wind sounded like music to the comfortable beings inside.

The Mistress drowsed over her book by the fire. Bruce snored snugly in front of the blaze. The Master had awakened from his nap and was in the study, sorting fishing tackle and scouring a rusted hunting knife. Then came a brief lull in the gale. All at once, Bruce was wide awake. Growling, he ran to the front door and scratched at the panel.

Thinking some guest might be arriving whose scent displeased the collie, The Mistress called to The Master to shut Bruce in the study. Shut up that way, he would not insult the visitor by barking. Very reluctantly, Bruce obeyed the order. The Master shut the study door behind him and came into the living room, still carrying the half-cleaned knife.

Since no knock or ring followed Bruce's announcement, The Mistress opened the front door and looked out. Dusk was falling. But it was not too dark for her to see two dogs tearing at something—something that lay hidden from her view in the deep snow a hundred yards away. She recognized Rex and Wolf at once, and wondered what they were playing with. Then, from the depth of snow beneath them, she saw a feeble head rear itself—a beautiful head, though torn and bleeding—a head that waveringly lunged toward Rex's throat.

"They're—they're killing Lad!" she cried in stark, unbelieving horror.

Forgetful of her thin dress and slippers, The Mistress ran toward the three dogs. Halfway to the battlefield, The Master passed by her, running through the knee-high snow at record speed. The Mistress heard his shout. And at the sound of it, she saw Wolf slink away from the slaughter like a scared schoolboy. But Rex was too far gone in primitive murder-lust to obey the shout. The Master seized him by the collar and tossed him ten feet to one side.

Blind with rage, Rex came flying back to the kill. The Master stood blocking Rex's prey. So in his blind mania, the huge dog sprang at the man. The Master's hunting knife caught him squarely behind the left foreleg. With a final grunt, Rex passed out of life.

Later, The Master would mourn his slaying of the pet dog that had loved and served him so long. But for now, he had eyes only for the torn and unconscious body of Lad, lying huddled in the bloody snow. The Master lifted Lad in his arms and carried him tenderly into the house. There, The Mistress's light fingers dressed his hideous injuries. At least thirty-six deep wounds perforated the old, worn-out body. Several of these needed professional care.

The Master called a veterinarian, who grumbled about having to chug ten miles through the storm. But when The Master agreed to pay him three times his usual fee, the man finally agreed to come to the rescue. When he arrived, Lad was lying with his head in The Mistress's lap.

After looking over the unconscious dog, the vet said sharply, "I wish I'd stayed at home. He's as good as dead."

"He's a million times better than dead," denied The Master. "I know Lad. You don't. He's gotten into the habit of living, and he's not going to break that habit, not if the best care in the state can keep him from doing it. Now, get busy!"

"There's no reason for me to stay here," objected the vet. "He's—"

"There are plenty of reasons for you to stay here," gently contradicted The Master. "You'll stay here till Lad's out of danger—even if I have to steal your trousers and your car. You're going to cure him. And if you do, you can write your bill on the $100 war bond I'll give you."

Two hours later, Lad opened his eyes. He was swathed in bandages, and he was soaked in ointments. Patches of hair had been shaved away from his worst wounds. Digitalis was reinforcing his faint heartbeat. The old dog looked up at The Mistress with his one unbandaged eye. By a heroic struggle, he wagged his tail just once. He tried to greet her with his usual trumpeting bark of welcome. But the bark failed completely.

Later on, Lad tried to tell The Mistress the story of the battle. Very weakly, he "talked." As he related his adventure, Lad's tones dropped now and then to the shadow of a ferocious growl. Then they would rise again—but only to the level of a puppy-like whimper. Lad had done a grand day's work, and he wanted applause. He had suffered much, and was still in terrible pain. And now he wanted sympathy and petting. Soon he fell asleep.

Two weeks later, Lad was finally able to stand up. After two more, he was able to go outdoors without help. Then one warm, early spring morning, the vet declared him out of danger. The wounded dog was very thin and very shaky. His muzzle was snow white, and he had the air of an old, old man, whose weak body is kept going only by a regal dignity. But he was alive.

Slowly, Lad marched from his piano cave toward the open front door. Wolf—in disgrace for the past month—happened to be crossing the living room toward the veranda. The two dogs reached the doorway at the same time.

Very respectfully, almost cringing with fear, Wolf stood aside to let Lad pass. The father walked by without even glancing at his son. But the old collie's step was suddenly stronger and springier, and he held his magnificent head high.

For Lad knew he was still king!

AFTERWORD

About the Author

Writers are often most successful when they write about subjects that interest them the most. Although Albert Payson Terhune did not start off writing about dogs, he used his love of collies to build a successful writing career.

Terhune was born in northern New Jersey in 1872, and he lived there until he died in 1942. In fact, The Place is based on "Sunnybank," the family's country estate, which eventually became Terhune's permanent home. Located in Pompton Lakes, New Jersey, Sunnybank is now a public park, where visitors can see the graves of many of the dogs mentioned in Terhune's works, including Lad.

Terhune's father was a minister, and his mother was a writer of popular homemaking books. Terhune's first wife, Lorraine Bryson Terhune, died shortly after giving birth to the couple's only child. "The Mistress" is modeled after Terhune's second wife, Anice.

After graduating from Columbia University, Terhune worked from 1894–1914 as a reporter for a New York newspaper, *The Evening World*. He also found time to write several books, which enjoyed limited success. These books, however, were not about dogs.

While working as a writer, Terhune also bred collies at his New Jersey estate. One of these "Sunnybank collies" was named "Lad." Terhune called Lad "the greatest dog by far" of all the dogs he'd ever known. It was this remarkable collie that finally inspired Terhune to start writing stories about dogs.

At first, Terhune's stories were published in magazines. They gained great popularity among men, women, and children everywhere. Even soldiers and sailors stationed in Europe during and after World War I enjoyed reading about Lad. Finally, in 1919, Terhune published these stories as a single book, entitled *Lad: A Dog*. Lad was so successful that Terhune followed it with a number of sequels, including books about Wolf, Bruce, and Lochinvar, as well as Lad.

Since the major adventures described in Lad are based on true events, many readers wonder what happened to Lad after his final battle with Rex. In an afterword to the original edition, Terhune writes that, for two more years, Lad lived on as "king" of the Sunnybrook animals. "Then, on a warm September morning in 1918, he stretched out to sleep in the coolest and shadiest corner of the veranda. And, while he slept, his great heart very quietly stopped beating. He had no pain, no illness, none of the depressing features of extreme age. He had lived sixteen years—years rich in life and happiness and love."

Albert and Anice Terhune buried Lad, along with his honorary Red Cross award, close to the house that the collie had so faithfully loved and protected. And they marked the site with a small granite monument, engraved with the words: LAD—THOROUGHBRED IN BODY AND SOUL.

About the Book

"A thoroughbred dog is either the best dog on earth, or else the worst," The Master tells the Wall Street farmer. But no individual thoroughbred dog can be "the best"—not even Lad. For there will always be some dogs who are stronger, and some who are better at following hand signals. Some will have a more fashionable look, or win more prizes at fancy shows. But even if Lad isn't "the best dog on earth," it would be hard to imagine a better one. In fact, Lad has many qualities that make him seem almost human—or, perhaps, even more than human.

First of all, Lad is courageous. He overpowers a knife-wielding burglar who sneaks into the house at night. When a crippled child comes to stay at the Place, Lad overcomes his own fear of snakes to save the girl from being bitten. As a result, the collie receives a near-fatal dose of snake venom. Later on, he trees a sneaky thief, and tracks down a sheep rustler. Finally, Lad refuses to run away when attacked by the younger, more powerful Rex. Instead, the older dog bravely fights rival head-on, even as he cleverly leads him back to the house.

Lad is also fiercely loyal to his "gods"— The Mistress and The Master. When The Mistress is deathly ill, Lad refuses to budge from her bedroom door, even though people keep tripping on him, and digging their shoes "painfully into his flesh." Lad absolutely and unquestioningly obeys The Master's order to be quiet. In fact, Lad is so obedient that he holds in his barks for a full two weeks. He goes against his nature by neither growling nor barking at an intruder. Even after the burglar is captured, Lad continues to feel "very worried and unhappy. For in spite of all his own attempts at silence, the thief had made a tremendous amount of noise. The commandment 'Quiet!' had been broken. And, somehow, Lad felt to blame."

Lad takes seriously his role to protect and defend his gods. He saves The Mistress from drowning. And when Parker starts to kick The Master, Lad goes for the thief's jugular. In fact, the collie is so outraged by Parker's gesture that he will never forgive nor forget Parker for trying to insult his god. As The Master explains to Maclay, Lad "has a kick to punish. He would follow Parker through the Sahara desert, if he had to."

In addition to his fierce loyalty, Lad also demonstrates a gentle, patient, and loving nature. Although the collie has little interest in adult guests, he adores children, "as a big-hearted dog always loves the helpless." Lad risks his life—and almost dies—to protect a little girl from being poisoned by a copperhead snake. He tolerates being mauled and slapped by the spoiled Morty. Then, to prevent his young tormentor from stepping into the blazing fireplace, Lad suffers even more pain, when Morty starts beating Lad "with his fists, tearing at the thick fur, stamping upon the tiny white forepaws, kicking the ribs and stomach." Even as the flames singe the dog's fur, Lad stands firm, steadfastly protecting the ungrateful boy from the fire.

Lad adores The Mistress so much that he cannot bear to see her suffer. When they are reunited after being separated in New York City, Lad first tries to lick away his goddess's tears. Finally, swallowing his pride and dignity, he rolls over like a foolish puppy, "because it made The Mistress stop crying and start to laugh. And that was what Lad most wanted her to do." Lad is so sympathetic that he feels The Mistress's suffering; he also feels responsible for easing it. At a dog show, Lad's eyes darken "with sorrow over his goddess's unhappiness, which he longed to lighten." Although Lad thinks The Mistress is behaving irrationally, the devoted collie willingly follows her senseless, humiliating commands "without questioning, because The Mistress told him to. The knowledge of her mysterious sadness made him even more eager to please her."

Lad helps and protects all living creatures—not just humans. When his mate, Lady, is wrongly accused of destroying the Master's prized stuffed eagle, Lad growls at the Master, taking her punishment on himself. While Lady is away, Lad comforts and educates their unruly son. And during a winter thaw, Lad rescues Wolf from drowning in the lake. Even when

Wolf later joins Rex in attacking Lad, the old dog refuses to attack his own son. Instead, he merely dodges Wolf's attacks, or brushes him off to the side.

Benefiting from the instincts he has inherited from his wolf ancestors, as well as the training he has learned from humans, Lad combines knowledge with wisdom. He understands human words, such as "quiet." But he also understands unspoken emotions, such as sorrow and fear. More sensitive than many humans, Lad understands the complexity of the world around him. He uses all his senses— watching, feeling, touching, smelling, and listening to tone of voice. From the moment he first sees sheep, Lad's ancient instincts somehow inform him about how to herd those silly-looking, wooly creatures. In fact, as The Master explains, "Lad knows everything"— even that mud baths will draw out poisonous snake venom.

In contrast to Lad, many of the humans in the story behave foolishly. They assume that Lad is vicious, wild, or untrustworthy. The mother of the girl threatened by the snake starts beating Lad before finding out what has really happened. The woman misunderstands what she has seen, and then refuses to listen to her daughter's eyewitness account. Morty's father grabs The Mistress's treasured chair and tries to crack it over Lad's head—even though the dog has just saved his son's life. Titus Romaine is so prejudiced against dogs that he is blind to the fact that it is his hired man, not Lad, who has been stealing his sheep. Even The Master reacts too quickly when he notices that his prized stuffed eagle has been damaged. Instead of thoroughly investigating and thinking logically about the situation, the man jumps to conclusions, and wrongly punishes Lady for breaking The Law.

Some humans are not only ignorant and thoughtless, but also heartless and cruel. Unlike Lad, who fights to protect or defend, some humans seem to take sadistic pleasure in hurting others. In New York City, the gang of boys "joined happily in the chase" after Lad, hoping to see the police officer shoot and kill the dog. Then, as Lad makes his escape by swimming across the river, "a yell went up from the gang standing at the end of the pier. Bits of wood and coal began to shower the water all around him." The boys seem to find it entertaining to try to hit the dog and make him drown. In the courtroom, Parker is eager to slash Lad with the whip. "With true pleasure in inflicting pain," the vicious man lashes at the dog "with all his strength."

In contrast to the noble and trustworthy Lad, some humans will do anything to get what they want, even if it is only a bit of ribbon. At shows like the one in Madison Square Garden, dog owners risk their dogs' health and well being by crowding them into cages and exposing them to disease. To give their animals a winning, but unnatural appearance, these self-serving humans torture their dogs— just to win a cup. They brutally "pluck out all the gray hairs, one by one . . . rub harsh clay into their tender skin . . . [and] sandpaper the dogs' sensitive tails and ears." The owner of Champion Coldstream Guard is so desperate to win that he shamelessly cheats his fellow sportsmen by taping down his collie's ears. At the charity dog show, Glure not only spends nearly $10,000 to outdo his neighbors; he also stoops to rigging the requirements so that he can finally show off a first-prize trophy.

Some humans are so greedy and cruel that they are willing not only to cheat to get what they want, but also to murder. The only reason Lad breaks The Master's law is to protect the innocent. But humans break their own laws for purely selfish reasons. One thief throws a knife at Lad, hoping to kill him, just so he can steal things that belong to a fellow human being. Another throws poisonous meat at Wolf, hoping to break into The Place. And Parker slaughters innocent sheep as a cover, in order to rob the man who has hired him, trusted him, and vouched for him in court.

Lad is truly remarkable—certainly better than many dogs. In some ways, he is also better than many humans. His keen senses detect information that humans cannot see, hear, smell, feel, or understand. In educating Wolf, Lad, unlike many human trainers, uses "time, patience, firmness, wisdom, self-control, and gentleness." In contrast, "It is a rare human who is blessed with even three of these qualities. But since Lad was a dog, he possessed all six." Unlike humans, who "have such odd ideas of justice," this dog fights fairly, and only when necessary to protect the weak and innocent. Lad is courageous, loyal, gentle, patient, loving, wise, kind-hearted, heroic, and fair. In short, he is noble and pure—a true "thoroughbred in body and soul."